"Dance with me, Ashley," he demanded

Jake's voice was curiously strained, and Ashley stared at him.

Barbara was obviously surprised by her fiancé's unexpected behavior, although she said nothing. Ashley was trembling, but Jake was at her side now, looking down at her with those brooding gray eyes, forcing her to obey.

The dance floor was crowded. "What on earth made you do a thing like that?" she asked forcefully. "Your fiancée is furious!"

Jake said nothing for a few moments, drawing her into the anonymity of the center of the floor. Then he bent his head and rested his forehead against hers and said quietly, "Because I had to. Because if I hadn't got you to myself soon, I think I'd have gone quietly out of my mind!"

ANNE MATHER
is also the author of these

Harlequin Presents

and these

Harlequin Romances

Many of these titles are available at your local bookseller.

For a free catalogue listing all available Harlequin Romances
and Harlequin Presents, send your name and address to:

HARLEQUIN READER SERVICE
1440 South Priest Drive, Tempe, AZ 85281
Canadian address: Stratford, Ontario N5A 6W2

ANNE MATHER

witchstone

Harlequin Books

TORONTO • LONDON • LOS ANGELES • AMSTERDAM
SYDNEY • HAMBURG • PARIS • STOCKHOLM • ATHENS • TOKYO

Harlequin Presents edition published September 1975
ISBN 0-373-10110-4

Second printing October 1977
Third printing June 1978
Fourth printing March 1980
Fifth printing January 1981
Sixth printing July 1981

Original hardcover edition published in 1974
by Mills & Boon Limited

Printed in Canada

CHAPTER ONE

THE frosty afternoon sunlight was casting a final mellow glow over the rooftops as Ashley Calder turned into Bewford's High Street and saw the small hotel ahead of her. Already it signified home, and unconsciously her step quickened as she thought of the glowing fire which would be burning in the grate of her aunt's living room and the homely smell of baking which always drifted from the kitchen. This was something she had never been used to. She had been too young when her mother died to remember much of what had gone before, and although her father had done his best, their home had lacked a woman's touch.

The Golden Lion Hotel was a stone-built, attractively weathered building that blended well with the row of tall, somewhat old-fashioned shops of which it was an integral part. It had a history, too. It was said that once some prominent member of an exiled royal family had taken refuge there on his journey north to Scotland and safety, and although much of the building had been renovated it still maintained that aura of the past that was so evident in knotted floors and low oak beams. In the few weeks she had lived there, Ashley had already acquired a sense of attunement with the place. She loved history and she was beginning to find her memories of her life in London less painful to contemplate. Her aunt and uncle had been so kind to her, sharing her grief over the sudden death of her father, and making her feel as much a part of their family as her cousins, Mark and Karen, that the future which had looked so black eight weeks ago was beginning to have possibilities again.

All the same, it had been quite a wrench leaving London, leaving everything and everyone she had ever really known to come north to Yorkshire to live with an aunt and uncle she could scarcely remember. She had met them once before, when she was five years old. But that was twelve years

5

ago now, the time when her mother had died and her sister and her husband had come south for the funeral. She had been too young then to appreciate any family differences, but as she grew older she sensed the antagonism her father felt towards her mother's sister. In any event, he had not encouraged Ashley to keep in touch with them, and distance had lent detachment. It was only now, after the kindness they had shown her since being informed of her father's death, that Ashley had begun to wonder why her father had not wanted her to get involved with them. Perhaps he had been afraid they would take her away from him, she mused. Perhaps he had sensed that the quality of their life was so much warmer, and that Ashley might have responded to it, used as she was to a somewhat emotionless existence.

Now Ashley shook her head. Surely her father had not believed that she would leave him alone. She would never have done that. She had loved him too much, even if sometimes she had suspected that she could never take the place of her mother in his affections.

But that was in the past now. Her future was here, in Bewford, and she swung lightly through the arched entrance to the cobbled yard at the back of the small hotel.

Her aunt was in the kitchen and looked up smilingly as Ashley came through the door bringing a chill gust of cold air with her. 'Hello, love,' she greeted her. 'Have a good day?'

'Hmm.' Ashley came over to where Mona Sutton was spreading lemon icing over a batch of small cakes. 'Can I have one of these, Aunt Mona?'

Her aunt raised a resigned eyebrow. 'I suppose so. Though where you put it all, I don't know.' She surveyed her niece's slender figure with a shake of her head. 'Aren't you afraid you'll get fat? Heavens, Karen only has to look at cakes and pastry and the inches seem to appear by magic!'

Ashley chuckled, swallowing the rest of the lemon sponge with obvious enjoyment. 'I'm just lucky, I guess.'

'Yes.' Her aunt sounded less than convinced. In her opinion Ashley's slenderness owed more to lack of food than anything else. When she first arrived in Bewford,

Mona had been appalled at how thin she was, and only now, after several weeks of good wholesome food, was she beginning to have a bit of flesh on her bones. 'Did you tell Miss Kincaid about the job at the library?'

Ashley unbuttoned the thick duffel coat she was wearing, throwing back the hood so that the heavy swath of corngold hair tumbled in disorder about her oval face. Then she perched on the edge of one of the draining units and said: 'Yes, I told her.'

'And what did she say?' Mona stopped what she was doing to look at her.

Ashley shrugged. 'I think she was disappointed.'

'Oh, Ashley!'

'Well, I know she hoped I'd go on to university——'

'So why don't you?' Mona stared at her.

Ashley bent her head. 'Do you want me to?'

'Love, it's not for me to say. It's what you want to do that matters. You know there's no question of a money problem. The money your father left is more than enough to pay for your education——'

'I know,' Ashley sighed.

'Don't you want a career?'

'Being a librarian is a career.'

'I know that. But, Ashley, you're only seventeen and already you've got three "A" levels. That certainly means something.'

'It means I swotted harder than everyone else . . .'

'No, it doesn't.' Mona wiped her hands on her apron. 'It means that you've got a damn good brain. And I know your father would expect you to use it to your best advantage.'

'Yes, my father would,' Ashley nodded. Then she looked at her aunt. 'Aunt Mona, will you tell me something?'

'If I can.'

'Why—why did I never see you in—in those years after—after Mummy died?'

Mona sighed. 'Oh, I don't know. We lived so far apart, I suppose,' she said quickly.

'Was that all it was?'

'What else could there be?'

'I'm asking you, Aunt Mona.'

7

Mona looked uncomfortable now. 'Ashley, it's all in the past, and your father's dead——'

'So?'

'Oh, child!' Mona made a helpless gesture. 'Your father was a good man. He did his best for you. He did his best for Delia—your mother.' She paused. 'But—well, he was a possessive man. At least so far as Delia was concerned. She and I—well, we'd been pretty close before she got married, but afterwards—your father didn't encourage us to meet. He wanted her all to himself.' She shook her head. 'Then they had you. I thought that would make a difference, but it didn't. Your lives and ours rarely crossed. When Delia died, we did meet. We came to the funeral, as you know. We wanted to help him then—we even offered to have you if it would help at all. But he was furious at the suggestion. He said that you and he would manage, and I'm afraid he became as possessive with you as he had been with Delia.'

'And yet he never really wanted me around,' murmured Ashley wonderingly.

'Selfish people are sometimes like that,' said Mona quietly.

'Yes.' Ashley understood now.

Mona frowned. 'Ashley, tell me honestly—what do you want to do? About going to university, I mean.'

Ashley looked up. 'Honestly?' And at her aunt's nod, she went on: 'I want to stay here, with you—with Uncle David—with Mark and Karen. I—I don't want to go away.'

'Oh, Ashley!' Mona came towards her, putting her hands on the girl's shoulders. 'Do you mean that?'

'You've all been so kind to me,' Ashley explained gently. 'I love being here. I feel—at home.'

'This is your home.'

'So I'd rather get a job in Bewford and stay here.'

'But Bewford County Library isn't the same as working in some big complex——'

'It doesn't matter. I've always wanted to do library work, and if it doesn't work out—well, I can always go to university later, can't I? There's plenty of time.'

Mona nodded, her eyes unusually bright. 'Of course there is, love,' she agreed, turning away. Then, more briskly..

'Now, are you going to go and change out of those school clothes before tea?'

Ashley straightened. 'What time are we eating?'

Mona shook her head. 'Food again!' she scolded, good-naturedly. 'Well, let's see. It's half past four at present. I think I should have it on the table for five o'clock. Then your uncle can enjoy his meal before opening up. Mark won't be in until later. He had to go up to the Hall.'

Ashley nodded, moving towards the door into the hall. Mark was employed by the Setons who lived at Bewford Hall. They were the largest landowners in the district. County people, Aunt Mona called them, but she said it with a trace of affection. Like everyone else in Bewford they were concerned with the affairs of the community, a situation which Ashley sometimes found hard to accept, coming as she did from a district in London where it was possible not to know one's next door neighbour.

The staircase to the upper floor of the Golden Lion was narrow and twisting, and led to a landing from which all the bedroom doors opened. Once the small hotel had catered for an occasional paying guest, but in recent years the Suttons had needed all the rooms for their own use.

Ashley shared Karen's room. It was the largest of the bedrooms, the only one in fact which could accommodate twin beds. She had at first expected some resentment from her cousin, but fortunately Karen wasn't like that. She was a gregarious sort of girl, open and friendly, glad of someone of a similar age to talk to, and it was Ashley who sometimes wished that Karen went to bed to sleep instead of to gossip into the small hours.

Karen was a couple of years older than Ashley, but without her academic ability. She had left school at sixteen and now worked in the Post Office. She had a steady stream of boy-friends, most of whom Ashley had only heard about, although she had met Frank Coulter, the man of the moment. He worked in the local garage and had the reputation of being the local Casanova. From the first, Ashley had disliked him, although she had to admit that part of her repugnance towards him was due to the fact that he had once attempted to make a pass at her when Karen was out of the room. She had been quite angry at the time, and she hoped Karen would soon find someone more reliable.

Ashley had friends of her own at school, of both sexes, but no one special. She wasn't interested in the casual physical relationships indulged in by most of the girls she knew, and found more enjoyment in books and music than petting on some street corner.

In the bedroom she stripped of the navy skirt and cardigan, the white blouse and navy and red striped tie which formed the uniform of Bewford Grammar School before rummaging through a drawer and pulling out a pair of shabby jeans and a scarlet sweater. The jeans accentuated the slenderness of her body, the curving length of her legs, while the ribbed sweater drew attention to the rounded swell of her breasts.

As she brushed her hair, she pulled a face at her reflection in the dressing table mirror. She was used to her appearance and saw no particular virtue in long, slightly slanted green eyes or a warm, beautiful mouth with a full lower lip. She secured the heavy swath of hair with two elastic bands so that a coil fell over either shoulder and then with a shrug turned towards the door.

Her aunt was in the dining room laying the table for their evening meal, and Ashley automatically took the cutlery from her and began setting the places. Her aunt smiled and took the opportunity to relax for a moment, lighting one of the infrequent cigarettes she smoked throughout the day. She was throwing the match into the grate when her husband came through from the bar.

'Well, well,' he remarked mockingly. 'Is this all you've got to do?'

David Sutton was a man in his early fifties, tall and spare-framed, with thinning fair hair and twinkling blue eyes. He was the exact opposite of Mona, in fact, who was inclined to plumpness like her daughter, and whose hair and colouring were definitely dark.

Now Mona regarded her husband with impatience. 'You've got to be joking!' she retorted, casting a resigned look in Ashley's direction. 'You see! I can't even have a cigarette without being caught out!'

Ashley smiled. This good-natured badinage was something she had not experienced before coming to live with her aunt and uncle. Her father had taken life much more seriously, and when she had first come to Bewford she had been concerned at the apparent constant state of conflict between these two. But as time went by her concern gave way to amusement as she realised that their relationship was based on warmth and understanding and nothing they ever said to one another during these petty little arguments penetrated the strength of their real feelings.

David Sutton turned to Ashley then, saying: 'Do you think you could come and put some bottles out for me later on? We're running short on ginger ales and tonics, and I could do with a few bottles of stout in the bar.'

Ashley nodded eagerly. From time to time she re-stocked the shelves when her uncle was busy, although he wouldn't permit her to serve behind the bar. 'Of course. Do you want me to do it now?'

'No, later on will do,' replied her uncle, reaching for his pipe from his jacket pocket.

'I should think so, too,' exclaimed Mona. 'The lass has just got home from school. She's hungry, aren't you, love?'

Ashley wrinkled her nose doubtfully. Obviously her aunt had chosen to forget that not too long ago she had been chiding her for eating too much. Changing the subject completely, she turned to her uncle and said: 'I've decided to take that job at the library after Easter—if they'll have me.'

David looked up from filling his pipe. 'Have you?' He looked pleased. 'I'm glad.'

'Are you?' Ashley felt all warm inside. She lifted her shoulders and let them fall again, spreading her hands in an encompassing gesture. 'Well, so am I.'

Karen didn't finish work until five-thirty and by the time she got home Ashley and her aunt had usually finished the main washing up of the evening and the Golden Lion had opened its doors to its patrons. David had a couple of women who helped in the bar in the evenings and they arrived about six. They were two young married women, supplementing their husbands' income by working in the

11

evenings when their husbands could look after their children. Ashley didn't know them very well yet, but Mark had told her that the husband of one of them worked for the Setons, too.

Ashley looked forward to Mark coming home. They got along well together. Although he was twenty-eight he had not as yet shown any inclination towards marriage and seemed to find his young cousin quite adequate company. He had taken her to the pictures a couple of times, and once to a horse sale at a nearby estate. But mostly he seemed to find the horses more absorbing, and Ashley, with her own love of solitude and the fascination of academic things, could appreciate this. Perhaps that was why they got along so well – because they each had other interests.

Ashley was coming along the hall later than evening, her arms filled with the small bottles of soda water, dry ginger and tonic her uncle needed, when Mark came through the door which led from the cobbled yard at the side of the hotel. It had begun to snow earlier on and flakes glinted on his fair hair. Ashley started to say: 'Are you frozen——' when she saw that her cousin was not alone. Another man had followed him into the hotel, a man as dark as Mark was fair, with the kind of tan impossible to achieve in these northern climes.

Mark grinned. 'What's this?' he queried, indicating the bottles. 'Secret drinking?'

Ashley's lips twitched. 'Hardly. Your father needs them. Excuse me——'

'Wait!' Mark glanced round at his companion. 'This is my cousin, Jake. Ashley, I'd like you to meet Jake Seton.'

Ashley could have wished that Mark had waited until she had shed the load of bottles before introducing her to his friend, but it was too late now to do anything about it. Instead, she was forced to stand there and offer a greeting, her face almost as red as her sweater.

'Hello, Ashley!'

Jake Seton's voice was low and deep, his eyes disturbingly intent between the longest lashes she had ever seen on a man. But if his lashes were unusual, they were the only effeminate thing about him. He was tall, taller even than

Mark who stood a good five feet eleven in his socks, with a lean, yet powerful body. He was not handsome in the accepted sense of the word, but Ashley thought, even with her small knowledge, that there was little doubt that some women would find the deep-set eyes, the harsh planes of his cheekbones and the somewhat thin lips attractive. Sideburns grew lower than his earlobes, while dark hair lay thick and smooth against his head, brushing the collar of his suede jacket. He appeared to use no hair dressing and consequently it looked glossily healthy. She thought he looked about Mark's age, but she couldn't be sure. Either way, it was nothing to do with her.

Realising that she had been staring, she turned away in embarrassment, making some comment about her uncle waiting for the bottles, and she sensed, rather than saw, Mark and his companion go down the hall and enter the private lounge at the back. In the bar, David Sutton regarded her flushed cheeks with some amusement.

'What's happened to you?' he asked, putting the back of his hand against her forehead. 'You running a fever or something?'

Ashley unloaded the bottles on to the floor behind the bar and began stacking them on the shelves. 'Of course not,' she denied swiftly.

David looked down at her bent head. 'Well, someone's responsible for that or I'm a Dutchman!' he declared.

Sighing, Ashley rose to her feet. 'Mark's just come home.'

David frowned. 'So what did he say to you?'

'Nothing. He—er—he wasn't alone.'

'I see. Who was with him? Don't tell me he's brought some girl home!'

Ashley moved her shoulders reluctantly. 'No. It was a man, actually. Someone called – Jake Seton.'

And only as she said the words did realisation of his identity come to her. Seton was the name of the people who lived at Bewford Hall. Sir James Seton was Mark's employer. Jake Seton had to be some relation.

Her uncle was grinning broadly now. 'Oh, I'm beginning to see,' he chuckled, much to her annoyance. 'It was Jake who spoke to you, was it? Yes—well, the lassies get a bit hot and bothered when he's around.'

Ashley assumed a defiant stance, her thumbs tucked into the low belt of her jeans. 'Do they really? Well, I was just embarrassed, that's all.'

Her uncle nodded thoughtfully. 'Of course. You won't have met him yet. But you'll soon get used to seeing him. He and Mark are good friends in spite of the differences in their backgrounds. I hadn't heard that he was back.'

In spite of herself, Ashley was curious. 'Back?' she echoed.

'Yes. From Austria. Jake's been away about six weeks, I guess. A group of them went on a skiing holiday.'

'I see.' That explained the tan, she supposed. 'Well, do you need any more—bottles, I mean?'

David looked at the neat rows. 'I don't think so, love. You go and talk to Mark and Jake. Where's Karen?'

'She's gone out with Frank.'

Her uncle grimaced. He could have wished his daughter was more like Ashley when it came to choosing her friends. 'All right,' he said now. 'I'll let you know if I need you later.'

Ashley nodded, but when she left the bar she stood rather hesitantly in the hall, wondering whether she dared to go up to her room instead of having to join her aunt and the two men in the lounge. She was hovering near the foot of the stairs when her aunt came out of the lounge closing the door behind her, obviously on her way to the kitchen.

'Oh, there you are, Ashley,' she said, when she saw the girl. 'I'm just going to make some coffee. You go in there and speak to Mark and Mr. Seton.'

Ashley smoothed her fingers over the rounded knob at the end of the banister. 'I—er—I was just going upstairs, Aunt Mona,' she murmured.

Mona frowned. 'Why? What's wrong with you?'

'Nothing's wrong. I—well, I knew Mark had a guest, and I thought I'd go and read——'

'Oh, get along with you!' Mona clicked her tongue impatiently. 'It's only Jake! Go on into the lounge, and stop talking such nonsense. I shan't be long.'

Heaving a sigh, Ashley crossed the hall and opened the lounge door. Both Mark and Jake Seton were settled in the easy chairs at either side of the blazing fire. They looked relaxed and comfortable, and Ashley felt as though she was interrupting them when they looked up at her reluctant entrance.

Jake Seton got immediately to his feet, indicating his chair. 'Would you like to sit here?' he asked.

Ashley closed the door and quickly subsided into a smaller chair quite close by. 'No, really, thank you. I'm perfectly all right here.'

'Very well.'

Jake exchanged a glance with Mark and then resumed his earlier position. For a few awkward moments nobody said anything and whatever conversation had been going on before Ashley's entrance had clearly been broken up. Ashley shifted uncomfortably. She should have insisted upon going upstairs.

But then Jake drew out a slim case of cheroots and offered them to Mark, saying: 'Mark tells me you're still at school, Ashley.'

Ashley flashed a quick look in Mark's direction, but he was leaning forward to light his cheroot from the lighter Jake had proffered and didn't notice. 'Yes, I am,' she replied, rather tersely.

Jake lay back in his chair inhaling deeply on the tobacco. 'And what do you intend to do afterwards? Go on to university?'

Ashley tugged a strand of her hair. 'I don't think so. I—well, I shall probably take up library work. That's really what I want to do.'

'Library work,' considered Jake thoughtfully. 'Where? In Bewford?'

'As a matter of fact, yes.' Ashley didn't altogether care for this interrogation.

Jake nodded. 'You like it here, then? You come from London, don't you?'

'Mark seems to have told you an awful lot about me, doesn't he?' parried Ashley, feeling not unreasonably impatient.

15

Jake smiled then, a lazy attractive smile that seemed to attack her in that vulnerable region below her ribcage in a curiously disturbing way. 'Actually, he didn't tell me that,' he confessed charmingly. 'David—your uncle, that is—told me you were coming to live with them before I left for Grüssmatte.'

'Oh!'

Ashley dug her nails into the moquette upholstery of her chair arm, refusing to look at her cousin who she sensed was annoyed with her now. And as though to prove this point, Mark got to his feet just then and said: 'As Ashley seems averse to talking about herself for once, shall we have a drink? Jake—your usual?'

Ashley looked up. 'Your mother's making coffee!' she exclaimed.

'So?' Mark looked down at her penetratingly, and her eyes dropped before his. 'Is there any law which says we can't have both?'

Ashley didn't bother to reply and Mark opened the lounge door. 'Shan't be a minute, Jake.' He flicked his gaze to Ashley. 'If you get into difficulties with this monster, just yell.'

After the door had closed behind him, Ashley felt worse than ever. At least when Mark had been present the onus had not been upon her as it was now. Forcing herself to meet Jake Seton's somewhat amused gaze, she said: 'Do you like skiing, Mr. Seton?'

'Very much.' He inclined his head.

Ashley sighed, looking down at her probing fingers again. 'And is that all you do?'

'Ski?' Jake studied the glowing tip of his cheroot. 'I wonder what you would say if I said yes.'

Ashley looked up defensively. 'I shouldn't say anything. It's nothing to do with me.'

'Isn't it?' Jake's eyes were narrowed now and she couldn't read their expression. 'But I detected a note of cynicism in your voice.'

Ashley was taken aback. 'I think you're mistaken.'

Jake shrugged. 'Very well. If you choose not to pursue it.'

'Pursue what?'

He drew deeply on this cheroot again. 'You asked what else I did. In fact, I believe the question was—*if* I did anything else.'

Ashley moved uncomfortably, wishing she'd never started this. Changing the subject entirely, she said: 'It's very cold this evening, isn't it? Although I don't suppose you find it any colder than Austria——'

'Come and sit by the fire, then. You said you weren't cold earlier on,' he remarked.

Ashley shook her head. 'I—I meant outside.'

'I see.' He paused. 'Tell me, do you know Grüssmatte?'

'Grüssmatte?' For a moment she was all at sea.

'Yes, Grüssmatte. In Austria. You said you didn't expect I would find this climate any colder than Austria. I wondered how you knew I'd been in Austria.'

Ashley flushed brilliantly. 'Er—as a matter of fact, Uncle David told me.'

'Did he indeed?' Jake's eyes were intent between the thick lashes. 'And were you discussing me with your uncle?'

'I—no—at least, not really.' Ashley's nails were almost penetrating the moquette as the pressure increased.

'But you did listen when he spoke to you, didn't you?'

Ashley decided the only way open to her was attack. 'If you're trying to tie me up in knots by proving that I was discussing you with Uncle David——'

Jake lay back in his chair, his expression mildly indulgent. 'Now why would I do a thing like that?' he mocked. 'You seem perfectly capable of doing it for yourself.'

To Ashley's relief, Mark chose that moment to re-enter the room. 'Oh, good,' he exclaimed. 'You're talking to one another. I had visions of a pitched battle being waged in my absence.'

'Don't be silly, Mark!' Ashley was curt. 'What's this?'

Mark was handing her a tall glass laced with ice cubes, and he grinned. 'Taste it! I think you'll like it. It's just potent enough to give the lemonade a kick.'

Ashley sipped the liquid experimentally. It was delicious, but she couldn't recognise the flavour.

'I think it looks like Advocaat,' remarked Jake, swallowing a mouthful of the amber liquid Mark had given him.

'It is,' agreed Mark, subsiding into his armchair again with a tall glass of lager. 'A golden drink for a golden girl!'

'Mark!'

Ashley felt more embarrassed than ever, but as her aunt arrived with the coffee she was saved the need of having to parry any further comments from either of them. Conversation became general and it was not noticeable that Ashley played very little part in it. She was content to sit in her chair and drink her coffee and remain silent, absorbed as she was with her own thoughts.

CHAPTER TWO

ASHLEY was almost asleep when Karen came noisily into the bedroom and switched on her bedside lamp.

'Ashley?' she hissed in a stage whisper. 'Are you awake?'

Ashley sighed. She had thought that for once Karen would see that her eyes were closed and not disturb her, but she should have known better. Rolling on to her back, shading her eyes with her arm, she said: 'Do you realise it's almost half past eleven, Karen? I'm tired. What do you want?'

Karen gave an apologetic smile. 'Sorry, love. I really thought you were awake.'

'I was,' admitted Ashley. 'What is it?'

'I just wanted to talk to you,' exclaimed Karen, beginning to get undressed. 'Guess what? Frank's got a new car!'

Ashley raised her eyes towards the bedroom ceiling. 'Super! Is that all?'

'Don't you want to know what it is?' Karen sounded disappointed.

Ashley gave a resigned gesture. 'All right. What is it?'

'It's a Triumph Spitfire. A gorgeous little sports car, and can it move! We went for a run in it this evening, and it was thrilling—really thrilling!'

Ashley blinked. 'Great. Have you just got back?'

'Well, I've just got in,' replied Karen insinuatively. 'We got back about half an hour ago.'

'Fine.' Ashley rolled on to her side again. 'Can I go to sleep now?'

'I suppose so.' Karen plumped down on to the side of her bed to take her tights off. 'What did you do this evening?'

'Nothing much.' Ashley's voice was muffled.

'Exciting!' Karen was sarcastic. 'Honestly, Ash, don't you ever get sick of staying in all the time? I mean, I'm sure Frank could fix you up with a blind date——'

'No, thanks!' Ashley turned so quickly that she pulled the blankets out of the side of the bed, and mumbled irritably as she pushed them in again. 'I don't need Frank Coulter to get dates for me. I'm perfectly capable of choosing my own boy-friends.'

Karen pulled on her pyjamas. 'So why don't you have any?'

'I do have friends,' protested Ashley.

'But you don't go out with them—at least, not alone any-way.'

Ashley sighed again. 'Look, you live your life and I'll live mine.'

'I just want you to have a little fun, that's all.' Karen clim-bed into bed. Propping herself on one elbow, she studied her cousin critically. 'You should, you know. You're very at-tractive.'

'Thank you.' Ashley wished she would hurry up and turn out the light.

'Don't you want to get married?'

'Oh, Karen, honestly!' Ashley had to smile. 'I don't want to get married for years yet! I'm not eighteen even. I intend to wait until—I'm—oh, I don't know—perhaps thirty, before I tie myself down with a home and children——'

'You're forgetting the most important part.'

'What's that?' Ashley frowned.

'A husband, of course. Or were you planning to have children and bring them up yourself?'

'Don't talk rubbish!' Ashley wrinkled her nose. 'You know what I mean. Besides, I may never get married.'

'No. That's true. But I want to. I've never been particularly interested in a career.'

Ashley nodded. 'And do you think this—association with Frank is serious?'

Karen shrugged. 'I don't know. Sometimes I think so, and then he does something or says something and—well, I won-der.' She drew the covers up to her chin, tipping her head on one side to look at her cousin. 'Mum said that Mark brought Jake Seton home with him this evening.'

Ashley was glad of the rose-shaded lamp to hide her colouring. 'Yes, that's right, he did.'

Karen rolled on to her side, facing her. 'What did you think of him?'

'Who? Jake Seton?'

'Who else?' Karen's tone was dry.

'I—er—he seemed very nice——'

'Nice!' Karen gasped. 'Love, a man like Jake Seton could never be described as—nice!'

'Why?' Isn't he?'

Karen gave an exasperated snort. 'Ashley! If you mean is he charming—intelligent, friendly, even, then—yes. I suppose in those terms, he is—nice. But that wasn't what I meant. Didn't you think he was attractive? Oh, I know he's a lot older than you, but even so . . .'

Ashley hunched her shoulders under the bedcovers. 'Yes, I suppose he is,' she admitted reluctantly. A slight smile touched her lips. 'Why don't you marry him if you find him so devastating?'

Karen grimaced. 'Chance would be a fine thing! Heavens, you don't suppose I'd be bothering with someone like Frank if I seriously thought I stood any chance with Jake Seton, do you?'

'You can't love Frank, then,' declared Ashley forcefully. 'Or you wouldn't be interested in anyone else.'

'Yes but the Setons are something else,' exlaimed Karen defensively. 'I mean, they really are different. It's only that Jake and Mark have known one another since they were at school together, and Jake is always so friendly to Mum and Dad that makes him seem approachable somehow. The rest of the family aren't like him. Oh, they're friendly enough, I suppose, but in a different way—a less personal way, if you know what I mean. They're sort of—oh, you know— aloof—lords of the manor—that sort of thing. They know everyone, of course. They speak to everyone. But you're always conscious of the gulf between them and us—it's a social barrier somehow.'

Ashley was intrigued now in spite of her tiredness. 'And you say—Jake Seton went to the same school as Mark?' she asked.

'Only for a short time,' answered Karen, rubbing her nose thoughtfully. 'Jake's a couple of years older than

21

Mark, but he did attend the County Infants for three years before going on to prep school. I don't know how they became friends, but they did—and it's stuck—which says a lot for Jake, actually. I don't think his family approve. So far as they're concerned, this is one of the local pubs, and if Jake comes here they put it down to the alcohol on the premises, not the company.'

'And—and Jake is a son of Mark's employer, is that right?'

'Not *a* son, love, *the* son! He has two sisters, but no brothers. Sir James Seton is his father. I suppose Jake will inherit the title one day. His name is James, really, but he's always been called Jake to avoid confusion.'

'I see.' Ashley digested this. 'I'm surprised he's not married.'

'He will be soon.' Karen's mouth turned down at the corners. 'The social occasion of the year is planned for the last week in June.'

Ashley frowned. 'What do you mean? He's getting married?'

'Naturally.' Karen expelled her breath noisily.

Ashley suddenly found the conversation rather boring. 'Oh, well,' she said shortly, 'you'll just have to make do with Frank, won't you?'

Karen watched her cousin roll herself in the covers and prepare herself for sleep. 'I suppose so,' she agreed slowly. 'Don't you want to know who he's going to marry?'

'Not particularly.' Ashley was abrupt. 'Oh, Karen, for goodness' sake, put out the light. I'm tired. I want to go to sleep.'

During the next couple of weeks, Ashley thought very little about Jake Seton. The weather was unusually cold for early March with heavy falls of snow blocking the roads, disrupting bus and train services. The moorland farmers who gathered in the Golden Lion on market days talked incessantly of the shortages of animal foodstuffs and the difficulties of lambing in these conditions. Ashley herself seemed to spend her time hurrying from home to school and then home again, and felt no desire to go out in the evenings as Karen did.

One afternoon, when a watery sun was fighting a losing battle with the freezing temperatures, she was walking home from school with a girl-friend when a sleek, dark green sports car slid to a halt beside them. They were scarcely a hundred yards from the school and at first Ashley thought it was someone who wanted directions. But then the nearside window was rolled down and she found herself looking into Jake Seton's face.

'Hello, Ashley,' he said, almost as if he had expected to see her. 'Can I give you a lift?'

Susan Knight, the girl who had been walking with her, drew back awkwardly, obviously recognising Jake, and Ashley felt embarrassed.

'I—we don't have far to go,' she replied briefly. 'Thank you all the same.'

Jake's lips thinned. 'I'm going that way anyway,' he said, thrusting open the door. 'Get in!'

There was such authority in his voice that Ashley found herself responding to it almost automatically, merely giving Susan an apologetic smile before stepping forward and climbing into the luxurious vehicle beside him. He leant across her to close the door with controlled firmness and for an instant she could smell the heat of his body and a faint trace of Havana tobacco, and felt the hardness of his arm against the softness of her breasts. Then the force of un-restrained power beneath the bonnet of the car was pressing her back in her seat as the car swept forward.

She had been in quite a number of cars during her com-paratively short life, but never one like this. Everything about it was smooth and expensive, and even without the scrawled identification along its side she would have guessed it belonged to some exclusive stable of custom-built sports cars.

Within seconds they had reached the end of Castle Lane and turned into the High Street, and Ashley's fingers tight-ened on her briefcase as he drew up outside the Golden Lion.

'Thank you,' she managed, and looked round for the door handle.

Without a word, Jake leant across her again and thrust open the door, and with a nervous smile she swung her legs out and stood up. She turned to close the door and found him sliding across her seat to climb out at her side, tall and disturbing in a black leather battle jacket over black suede trousers.

'Well?' he challenged, looking down at her, and she detected impatience in the word. 'That wasn't so bad, was it?'

'No.' She looked down at the toes of her shiny black boots.

'But you didn't want to ride with me, did you?'

'No.'

'Why not?' He was clearly perplexed.

'I—Susan had to go home alone.'

'That was Tom Knight's girl, wasn't it?'

'Yes.'

'Then, as I recall it, they live along Westbrook Terrace. She was about to turn along Westbrook Gardens, which is not your way at all.'

Ashley looked up at him. 'How do you know?'

'Her father used to work for us.'

'Oh, I see.' Ashley resumed her contemplation of her toes.

'So would you like to tell me the real reason why you didn't want me to give you a lift?'

Ashley looked round. The Golden Lion was in a prominent position in the High Street and standing here beside the unmistakable lines of the sports car they were attracting quite a lot of attention from late afternoon shoppers.

'Oh, please,' she began. 'I—I expect I was surprised to see you there, that's all. Look, I'm freezing standing here. Are—are you coming in?'

'Are you inviting me?' His eyes probed hers with disturbing intensity.

'Me?' exclaimed Ashley ungrammatically. She moved her shoulders helplessly. 'Isn't it Mark you've come to see?'

'So far as I am aware, Mark is at work,' replied Jake

easily, his thumbs tucked into the low belt of his pants.

Ashley was at a loss to know what to do. She wasn't used to dealing with men, and particularly not with a man like Jake Seton. She shifted her weight uncomfortably from one foot to the other, not knowing what to say. Then, as though taking pity on her, or perhaps it was simply that he was tired of waiting for her to make a move, Jake suddenly shrugged his broad shoulders and with a slight bow of his head walked round his car and swinging open the door climbed behind the wheel. There was a slight squeal of protest from the tyres as he drove away, but Ashley scarcely registered it, her heart was pounding so loudly.

Her aunt was in the kitchen as usual when she entered the hotel, and gave her niece a surprised look. 'You're home early,' she exclaimed. 'Is it snowing again?'

Ashley shook her head, turning away to get herself a drink of water from the tap. 'No. No—I got a lift actually.'

There was silence for a moment as she swallowed half the glass of water, but when she turned back to her aunt she saw she was waiting for further explanations.

'It was Mr. Seton. He gave my a lift.'

Mona Sutton raised her eyebrows. 'Jake?'

'That's right.' Ashley unbuttoned her duffel coat. 'I'll go and get changed——'

'Wait a minute!' Mona bent to take a tray of sausage rolls out of the oven. Putting them down on top of the cooker, she added: 'What did he say?'

Ashley shrugged. 'Nothing much.'

Mona sighed. 'He must have said something. How did he come to give you a lift?'

'I don't know.' Ashley fidgeted with the toggle fastenings of her coat. 'Susan and I were just walking along when—when he stopped. And offered.'

Mona frowned. 'And where is he now?'

'I expect he's gone home.' Ashley turned towards the door.

Mona clicked her tongue. 'I wonder why he didn't come in. It's not like Jake to be in the vicinity and not call. Oh, well . . .' She began lifting the sausage rolls on to a wire tray to cool. 'Perhaps he was in a hurry.'

'Perhaps he was,' agreed Ashley quickly, and went out of the door before her aunt could say anything else. She didn't want to talk about it.

But in her room the incident could not be dismissed so lightly. She knew that Jake's reasons for not coming into the hotel had had to do with her attitude, and she couldn't help feeling a little guilty. After all, she had absolutely no reason to behave towards him as she had, and she knew that the rest of the family would not be at all pleased if they discovered the way she had reacted to his kindness.

As she changed out of her school clothes into her usual attire of jeans and a sweater she tried to find excuses for herself. He made her feel uneasy, unsure of herself, and the knowledge that everyone else regarded him with what she felt was an unwarranted show of affection irritated her. He was only a man when all was said and done, and just because his name was Seton it did not make him some kind of god in her eyes. Besides, she didn't want to have to feel grateful to him for anything.

During their meal that evening Mark volunteered the information that Jake had been away for the day. 'There's some talk about selling that land where the old sawmill used to be,' he said. 'I think Jake went to Leeds to find out about conditions of tenure, development—that sort of thing.'

Mona looked up with interest. 'Oh, then that's where he'd been when he picked Ashley up,' she decided.

'Picked Ashley up?' Mark was puzzled. 'What are you talking about?'

'He gave your cousin a lift home from school this afternoon,' explained his father.

Mark looked at Ashley in surprise. 'Did he? That was kind of him.'

'Yes, wasn't it?' Mona smiled comfortably. 'But he didn't come in. I expect he wanted to report back to Sir James.'

'Yes,' Mark nodded. 'Well, Ashley? What did you think of the Ferrari?'

Ashley shrugged, determinedly keeping her eyes on her plate. 'Is that what it was? I didn't notice,' she lied.

26

Mark chuckled, shaking his head. 'It's just as well it was you and not Karen he gave a lift to. She'd have been making some big thing of it by now.'

They all laughed and Ashley forced herself to join them. But she wasn't at all happy about the situation, and she half hoped Jake would come to the hotel that evening so that she could assure herself that he had not taken offence at her words.

However, Jake did not come to the hotel that evening or indeed for almost a week, and each succeeding day that passed made Ashley more than ever convinced that she was responsible for his absence. She was tempted to ask Mark whether he had spoken to his employer's son, but she could hardly do that without attracting attention to herself so she had to wait in impatience, hoping for the best.

Then, six days later, she was stretching up to fasten a new bottle of vodka into its place in the wall fitment behind the bar when a voice she was programmed not to forget said: 'Is the amount of flesh you're exhibiting designed to increase the thirst of your customers?'

Ashley swung round abruptly, hastily pulling down the short green sweater which had ridden up leaving a smooth expanse of midriff bare. Jake was seated on one of the tall stools at the bar, and she smoothed her hands down over her hips nervously, conscious of a disquieting sense of pleasure in just seeing him there. The bar was quiet at this hour of the evening and her uncle had left her in charge for once while he went down to the cellar to bring up some crates of beer.

'Good evening, Mr. Seton,' she greeted him politely.

'Hello, Ashley.' He inclined his head. 'How are you?'

'Oh—oh, I'm fine.' Ashley's fingers gripped the bar very tightly. 'Can I get you a drink?'

'I thought your uncle didn't permit you to serve drinks.'

Ashley flushed. 'He's not here right now——'

'No. I had noticed.' His tone was dry as he drew out a case of cheroots and put one between his teeth. 'Leave it. I can wait until David gets back.'

Ashley sighed as he lit the cheroot, pushing her fingers into the hip pockets of her jeans. The fact that he was right,

27

that her uncle did not approve of her attempting to serve customers, irritated her. It was annoying always to be treated as a schoolgirl—even though she still was one. But she would be eighteen in a month, and some girls were already married at that age.

Jake studied her mutinous expression tolerantly. 'Don't frown so. I'm not in any hurry.'

Ashley made no reply, turning away to take a cloth and dust the glass shelves behind the bar. She was tempted to ask him why he hadn't been into the hotel before this, but it was not up to her to question his movements.

'Tell me,' he said suddenly, 'do you have to go to the Grammar every day? I thought Mark told me you'd already passed your exams.'

Ashley straightened, her green eyes mirroring her surprise. 'I don't *have* to go,' she admitted. 'But as I'll be leaving soon ...' She shrugged awkwardly.

'I see.' Jake looked down to flick ash into the tray. 'Do you feel like taking a day off?'

Ashley stifled a gasp. 'A day off?' she echoed. 'W-why?'

Jake continued to take an immense amount of interest in the burning end of his cheroot. 'I thought you might like to come to a sale with me on Thursday,' he said quietly. 'It's at a country house in Swaledale. As I understand it, they have a particularly good library.'

Ashley put down the cloth she had been holding and stared disbelievingly at his bent head. 'Why—why are you asking me?' she got out.

He looked up then, and she saw his eyes were grey, not black as she had at first imagined. 'Because I thought you'd be interested,' he replied. 'Are you?'

Ashley moved awkwardly. 'I—well, yes—of course I'm interested. But——'

'But what? I'll ask your uncle if you want me to. It's a perfectly harmless invitation. I don't think he'll object.'

Ashley glanced over her shoulder. 'Perhaps not.'

'Well? Do you want to come or don't you?'

Ashley shook her head. 'Who else will be going?'

'Who else?' Jake looked impatient. 'No one else, why?'

Ashley sighed. 'I don't understand why you should want

to take me.' She moved her shoulders helplessly. 'Particularly after—after——'

'After what?' Jake's eyes were intent. 'After the way you spoke to me the last time we—met?'

'Well—yes.'

'I don't hold grudges.' He drew deeply on his cheroot. 'Do you?'

'I don't know.' Ashley was uncomfortable. 'What—what will people say?'

'People?' His lips were drawn in now.

'Yes, people,' she insisted, spreading her hands. 'Look, I know I don't know Bewford as well as you do, but I have noticed how people talk.'

'And how will they find out?'

Ashley's eyes widened. 'My uncle and aunt will know.'

'All right.' His eyes narrowed. 'Don't tell them.'

Ashley felt the first twinges of alarm. 'Are you serious?'

'If you've got qualms, don't tell them.' Jake sounded bored.

'But—but I couldn't *not* tell them.'

'That's up to you, isn't it?'

'Don't you care?'

'Not particularly.'

Ashley turned away. She felt almost sick with reaction. She had no idea what his real thoughts on the matter were or whether he wanted her to tell anyone or not. And she simply wasn't the type to lie to her aunt and uncle about something so important. How could she pretend to be going to school as usual when in fact she intended going away for the day with Jake Seton? She drew in a deep breath. He shouldn't have asked her. He shouldn't have placed her in such a position. She hadn't the experience to deal with it.

Taking another breath, she turned back to him just as her uncle came into the bar carrying two crates of light ale.

'Hello there, Jake,' he exclaimed warmly, when he saw who was seated at the bar. 'Long time, no see. Ashley been looking after you, has she?'

Jake nodded. 'How are you, David?'

Ashley's uncle pushed the crates of ale beneath the bar with his foot. 'I'm all right, I suppose,' he answered with a grin. 'I'll be better when this weather improves a bit. Still, at least the snow seems to have disappeared at last.'

Jake stubbed out his cheroot. 'Yes. Things are getting back to normal.'

'Have you been away?' Clearly David Sutton had no qualms about querying Jake's prolonged absence.

'As a matter of fact, I have.' Jake rested his elbows on the bar. 'There were a couple of functions I had to attend in London, and Barbara had some shopping to do, so we were away three days.'

Barbara! Who was Barbara? Ashley stood slightly behind her uncle wondering whether she could be one of the sisters Karen had mentioned. Or was she his fiancée? After their conversation of a few moments ago, it was all rather unpalatable somehow. How could he sit there and blithely talk about the things he had been doing when only minutes before he had asked *her* to spend a day with him? Or was she of such little importance that he could dismiss her in much the same way as he would a child?

Her uncle seemed to remember she was still there and turned to her. 'You can get along now, Ashley,' he directed with a smile. 'Thanks for keeping an eye on things while I was away.'

He turned back to add a couple of cubes of ice to a glass containing a generous proportion of whisky which he pushed across the bar to Jake as Ashley moved towards the door which led into the hall at the back of the hotel. Was that all? she thought dully, aware of an intense feeling of disappointment now that it seemed that all chance of spending the day with Jake was slipping out of her grasp. Wasn't he even going to mention the invitation again?

She glanced back once and her eyes met his over the rim of the glass he had raised to his lips. There was an enigmatic gleam in the grey depths and she thought there was silent mockery there too. She quickened her step and had reached the doorway when he called: 'Are you coming to Raybury with me on Thursday, Ashley?'

She halted, and swung round, her eyes going to her uncle, who had stopped what he was doing to raise his eyebrows. 'What's this?' he asked, frowning.

Jake swallowed another mouthful of his whisky before saying: 'I've invited Ashley to come to a sale with me on Thursday—in Swaledale. It's the Fallow House at Raybury.'

Ashley supported herself against the door jamb. 'I—I don't know whether I should go, Uncle David,' she murmured unevenly. 'Wh-what do you think?'

David Sutton was clearly unprepared for such a question. 'Well, I don't know, lass,' he admitted, his gaze flickering doubtfully towards Jake. 'You do have your school work to think of . . .'

Jake finished his whisky and toyed with the glass. 'One day more or less won't make a lot of difference, will it?' he commented. 'Ashley says she's leaving soon anyway.'

'That's true.' David looked troubled. 'All the same, perhaps you should ask your aunt, Ashley. She's better equipped than me to decide these things.'

Ashley hesitated, aware of the deepening twist to Jake's mouth. Obviously he considered the whole affair unnecessary and childish. What was he asking, after all? Just a few hours of her time—and for her benefit. She would love the opportunity to wander round the library of some old house.

'I would like to go, Uncle David,' she asserted, making a decision. 'And taking a day from school presents no problems.'

David shook his head. 'Well, I suppose it's for you to say,' he murmured. He looked at Jake. 'Why do you think this sale will interest Ashley?'

Jake pushed his glass towards the other man, indicating that he would like another. 'She likes books—libraries. As I understand it, there's quite a comprehensive library for sale.'

David measured more whisky into Jake's glass. 'I see.' He picked up the ice tongs. 'And how far is this place—Raybury?'

'Fifty—maybe sixty miles. It's near Richmond. I should think Ashley would enjoy seeing something of the countryside around here.'

David handed him his glass again. 'No doubt,' he conceded dryly. 'Well, lass, are you going?'

31

Ashley nodded. 'If you don't mind.'

Her uncle gave her an impatient look before turning back to Jake. 'What time do you expect to leave?'

'I thought about nine-thirty, if that's all right with you.' He looked towards Ashley, and she nodded, bending her head to avoid the piercing penetration of his eyes. 'The sale's not till noon, but we can look round beforehand.'

Ashley felt an unwilling sense of excitement. She couldn't help it. It was all so totally unexpected, and after the way she had been worrying about Jake Seton this week it was doubly tantalising. But she forced herself to calm down, feeling angry that she should be getting so heated over something which he obviously regarded with little concern. It was just an auction sale, when all was said and done, with a lot of musty old books to browse through, and that was why he was taking her.

Leaving the bar, she made her way to the lounge where her aunt was sitting knitting. Both Mark and Karen were out for the evening and Mona looked up smilingly when Ashley entered the room.

'Come in, love,' she greeted her. 'Has your uncle finished in the cellar?'

'Yes.' Ashley subsided into the armchair opposite. 'It's cosy in here, isn't it?'

'Hmm.' Her aunt bent to take another ball of wool from her knitting bag. 'You can put the television on if you'd like to.'

'No, thanks.' Ashley crossed her legs, swinging one foot restlessly.

Mona looked at her. 'You seem distracted. Is something wrong?'

Ashley coloured. 'No, nothing.' She reached for a magazine and flicked through its pages without interest. Then, taking the bull by the horns, she said: 'Would you mind if I took a day off school on Thursday?'

Mona's busy fingers stilled. 'Why? What do you want to do?'

'I—I've been invited out for the day,' said Ashley carefully.

Mona looked surprised. 'Invited out? Who by?'

'Actually—Jake Seton.'

There, it was out. Ashley closed the magazine and sat with her hands curled tightly on top of it.

'With Jake?' Mona was clearly perplexed. 'When—that is—how have you spoken to him?'

She didn't appear angry at the news and Ashley gathered confidence. 'He was in the bar just now. There—there's a sale of some old house at Raybury——'

'Raybury?'

'Yes. And as there's a library, he thought I might be interested in going with him.'

Mona began to knit again. 'Really? And what did you say?'

'Well, at first I wasn't sure—but then, after I'd spoken to Uncle David, I said yes.' Ashley looked anxious. 'Do you mind?'

Mona shook her head helplessly. 'Why should I mind?' She looked up again. 'I suppose it was kind of him to ask you. Did you—that is—you didn't insinuate——'

Ashley's colour deepened again. 'I knew nothing about it until he mentioned it,' she denied fiercely. 'Oh—oh, I wish I'd never said I'd go now!'

'Why?' Mona put her knitting aside. 'Don't be silly! I'm sure you'll have a lovely day. Is Miss St. John Forrest going, too?'

'Miss St. John Forrest?' Ashley was at a loss. 'Who's that?'

'Jake's fiancée—Barbara. Barbara St. John Forrest. Haven't you heard her name mentioned?'

'I don't think so.' Ashley shook her head, but as she did so she remembered a few minutes ago, in the bar, when Jake had mentioned that name and she had wondered whether it might be his sister.

'But you did know he was engaged?' Mona was adding. 'Didn't you?'

'Yes. Karen told me.'

Mona seemed satisfied with this news. 'Good. Well, you'll have to speak to Miss Kincaid tomorrow and tell her you won't be in on Thursday, won't you?'

'I suppose so.'

Ashley sounded less than enthusiastic and her aunt gave her a little impatient pat on her hand. 'Stop looking so depressed! Jake will look after you. And at least you can be sure of one thing—he wouldn't have asked you to go with him without mentioning it to Barbara first. Just go and enjoy yourself.'

Ashley opened the magazine again and tried to concentrate on a feature about making the most of your hair, but her mind wasn't on it. She was thinking of something her aunt had said—that Jake wouldn't ask her to go out with him without first discussing it with his fiancée.

This information should have pleased her—it should have reassured her that his invitation was considered and deliberate, and not a spontaneous impulse which might be regretted later. But instead, she felt raw and indignant, reluctant to be the unwilling recipient of his patronising generosity.

CHAPTER THREE

THEY had been climbing steadily for several miles, and when Jake suddenly pulled the car off the road into a parking area, Ashley saw that they were at the head of a steep bank which wound down into the valley. Spread out below them was a carpet of colours—trees and fields, scattered farms and close-knit villages, all dwarfed from this altitude. A faint mist still lingered to shroud the distant hills, but the sun was gaining strength by the minute and had already melted the rime frost from the hedgerows.

The engine of the car was suddenly silent and rather than look at her companion, Ashley looked about her. Even at this comparatively early hour there were motorists about, and several had parked here to buy hot drinks from a mobile caravan that stood a few yards away.

'Well?' said Jake unexpectedly. 'Have you nothing to say for yourself? You haven't opened your mouth since we left Bewford!'

Ashley was forced to glance round then, and she moved her shoulders indifferently, looking down at her hands clasped in her lap. 'I'm sorry. I just had nothing to say.'

'I see.' Jake's mouth had a sceptical curve. 'Do you want some coffee?'

Ashley looked towards the mobile caravan. 'If you'd like some, I'll have some——'

'Will you?' Jake sounded annoyed, and thrusting open his door he climbed out, slamming the door behind him so heavily that Ashley's head sang with the sound.

She watched him walk across to the caravan, tall and lean in close-fitting navy pants and a cream sweater. His hair looked particularly dark in the pale sunlight, and although it was bitterly cold still he seemed unaffected by it. He returned a few minutes later with two plastic cups and she leant across his seat to thrust open the door from the inside so that he could climb in again.

He handed her one of the steaming cups of coffee and she sipped the liquid gratefully. It was very comfortable in the warm car, looking out on the sunlit day, able to enjoy the scenery without suffering its less pleasant aspects.

Jake finished his coffee quite quickly, and putting the cup down lit a cheroot, exhaling the aromatic flavour of tobacco into the air. The silence between them seemed infinitely more pronounced now that the vehicle was stationary, and Ashley began to experience a feeling of nervous tension. She had never really been alone with a man before, and she couldn't help feeling apprehensive.

At last he half turned in his seat to look at her, and said: 'Why did you come with me? It's pretty obvious you're not enjoying yourself.'

Ashley looked down at her half empty cup of coffee. 'Why do you say that?' she parried.

Jake uttered an expletive. 'You know damn well why. I might as well be alone!'

Ashley felt terrible. 'I'm sorry.'

Jake shook his head impatiently. 'Are you?' He dropped ash from his cheroot into the tray provided. 'What I can't understand is—why did you agree to come? No one forced you. I just thought you might enjoy it. As it is, I doubt whether either of us is going to do so.'

Ashley shifted unhappily in her seat. 'I—did want to come.' she insisted.

'*Did* being the operative word, I suppose.'

'Yes—no—oh, no! That's not what I meant to say.' She looked at him helplessly, her green eyes slanted and appealing. 'I just think that—perhaps you shouldn't have asked me!'

Jake's eyes narrowed. 'Why not?'

'Well, I suppose because—because you're—well—who you are,' she murmured lamely.

'You mean because I'm so much older than you are—or because I'm engaged to be married—or because my father employs your cousin?'

Ashley coloured. 'A combination of all three, I suppose.'

'I see.' Jake took a long draw on his cheroot and then pressed it out with savage movements.

'You—understand, don't you?' Her voice was uneven.

'What's to understand? It all comes down to the same thing, doesn't it? You wish you hadn't come because you're bored——'

'That's not true!' Ashley's eyes were stormy now.

Jake made an impatient gesture. 'Then tell me what my age, my fiancée and my money has to do with us going to see a library fifty miles away?'

Ashley felt angry. He was deliberately misunderstanding her. He must know what she meant. 'Because I don't like being patronised,' she got out at last, trembling at her own temerity.

'Patronised?' Jake glared at her. 'Who's patronising you?'

'You are!' Ashley's nails bit into her palms. 'Whose idea was it to take me to Raybury? Yours—or your fiancée's?'

'My God!' Jake lay back in his seat in disbelief. 'What the hell are you talking about? You know whose idea it was—mine! It was conceived in the bar of the Golden Lion.'

Ashley took a deep breath. 'But why? Why me? Why not Karen, for instance?'

Jake hunched his shoulders. 'I've told you. Because I thought you'd find it interesting. I didn't realise there was going to be an inquest into my motives or I'd have had something prepared.'

Ashley stared unseeingly through the windscreen. 'I see.'

'Does that satisfy you?'

She shrugged. Did it? Was she satisfied now that she knew that Jake had not discussed his intentions with his fiancée before asking her out with him? She ought to be. And why did she need that reassurance anyway? She was trying to read more into his invitation than he had ever intended. And why? Because she was childish enough to want him to see her as an equal and not as a schoolgirl.

Jake swung round in his seat. 'I think we'd better get on,' he said shortly, 'unless you'd rather go back!'

Ashley bit her lips. 'Of course I don't want to go back,' she exclaimed, stretching out a hand impulsively towards him. His forearm was hard beneath her fingers, the muscles taut, the heat of his flesh tangible through the soft wool. 'Look, I know you'll probably think I'm stupid, but—well, Aunt Mona said that no doubt you had discussed the idea of inviting me with your—your fiancée, and I—I didn't——' She shook her head. 'Well, I didn't like the idea of being—discussed!'

'You mean I have Mona to thank for this?' he queried sarcastically, resting his elbows on the steering wheel.

Ashley's fingers probed his arm almost involuntarily. 'Are you—very angry?'

He looked down meaningfully at her hand and she hastily withdrew it, linking her fingers together in her lap again. 'I'm not angry—just irritated.' He sighed. 'I should perhaps point out that I do not have to clear my movements with Barbara. If I choose to invite you to accompany me to a sale—anywhere—that's my decision, and no one else's.'

Ashley bent her head, her hair falling like a silken curtain about her cheeks. 'If you say so.'

'Damn you, I do say so!' He turned the ignition with controlled violence. 'Shall we go?'

Ashley nodded, and the sleek sports saloon swung round in a circle to merge into the stream of traffic.

They drove down Sutton Bank and followed the winding road to Thirsk, entering the small market town just after ten-thirty. Ashley looked about her with interest. In spite of the fact that she and Jake were still saying little to one another, the atmosphere between them had significantly changed, and she no longer felt like an unwelcome encumbrance.

A few miles beyond Thirsk they joined the main trunk road north and for a while Jake had to concentrate on his driving. He controlled the powerful car expertly and without seeming effort, and Ashley was content to relax inside her seat belt and enjoy the ride.

They left the motorway just before Scotch Corner, taking the Richmond road for a short distance before turning off for Raybury. Traffic was sparse on these country roads, although they did pass one or two vehicles which Ashley thought might conceivably be on their way to the sale.

It was nearing eleven-thirty when they ran through the

village of Raybury, and Ashley was enchanted by the tall houses flanking the village green, and the ducks on the pond. Daffodils were blooming in clutches, and in spite of the cold the trees showed definite signs of new life.

'What a pretty place!' she exclaimed, and Jake glanced indulgently at her.

'You think so?'

'Hmm. Don't you?'

'Oh, yes, I like it,' he nodded. 'I used to come here a lot at one time. The father of one of my friends at university was the village doctor here. That was his house—there, can you see?'

He pointed to a tall white-painted building with the metal plate still on the tall gatepost, and Ashley leant forward to see, her arm brushing his.

'Oh, yes,' she smiled. 'Isn't he here any longer?'

Jake shook his head, as she sank back in her seat. 'Ben's father retired to Spain about five years ago, I believe, and Ben himself is married and lives in Scotland. He's a doctor, too.'

'And didn't you want a career?' asked Ashley impulsively, and then pressed a hand to her mouth as though to stifle the words.

Jake slowed to pass some children on bicycles. 'It depends what you mean by a career,' he replied, without rancour. 'I did get my degree, if that's any saving grace.'

Ashley looked apologetic. 'I'm sorry. It's none of my business.'

Jake's lips twisted. 'No, it's not, is it?'

'Do you mind?' Her eyes were challenging.

For a moment his gaze held hers and then he was forced to look back at the road. 'No,' he said quietly, 'I don't mind.'

It wasn't what he said, but the way he said it, that made something inside Ashley stretch and expand and send prickles of awareness out to the extremities of her body. He had such an attractive voice, she told herself, trying to analyse her enjoyment of his company. The simplest thing was made to sound as though it was for her ears alone, and to imagine him saying more intimate things caused a surge of unexpected heat to moisten her palms and dry her throat.

Oh, God, she thought suddenly, I'm enjoying this too much. It was only a casual outing, after all, with a definite purpose in mind, and she was imbuing it with attributes of a much more personal nature.

Fallow House stood behind a high brick wall at the end of the village. It was not a particularly attractive dwelling, made of grey stone, with several unsightly chimneys and a welter of outhouses tacked on to the main building with an absence of design or balance. There were several cars already parked when Jake brought the Ferrari to a smooth halt on the gravelled forecourt, and almost before he had opened his door a man came hurrying down the steps of the house towards him.

The newcomer was of medium height, which meant that Jake was much taller, and had a decided paunch beneath his well cut lounge suit. He looked about fifty, Ashley decided, and his wispy brown hair had been combed across the bald patch that was obviously the bane of his life. But he was certainly delighted to see Jake and shook hands with him warmly.

Pushing open her door, Ashley climbed out, shivering as a sudden gust of wind probed the buttoned fastening of the red blouse she was wearing. Flared cream slacks were warm against her legs, and she bent to pull her suede coat from the back of the car. The coat was dark green, edged with cream fur along the collar, cuffs and hem, and had a warm hood which she drew up over her ears.

Jake saw that she had got out, too, and excusing himself from the other man for a moment, pulled his own sheepskin jacket from the Ferrari. Then he locked the car and said: 'Shall we go inside? We can talk just as easily there.'

The smaller man nodded, his gaze flickering speculatively over the slim girl at Jake's side. Ashley wondered whether he knew Barbara and was perhaps conjecturing on her relationship with Jake.

There were quite a lot of people in the draughty hall of the house, standing about in groups talking, and Jake spoke to a number of them. Ashley got quite accustomed to being mentally appraised immediately after Jake had been greeted, but she couldn't help feeling slightly embarrassed by the closeness of their scrutiny. However, Jake seemed totally indifferent to their interest in his companion, and apart from introducing her to Walter Beswick, the man who had joined them on their arrival, he made no concessions to their curiosity.

Wandering round the house at Jake's side, listening to his conversation with the other man, Ashley gathered that there were several valuable pieces here among a rather motley assortment of old furniture. There was, for instance, a seventeenth-century walnut cabinet, with lots of small drawers decorated with floral marquetry; an Adam table carved with rams' heads that Ashley found quite fascinating; and a magnificent four-poster bed in the master bedroom, which according to the catalogue dated back to the eighteenth century.

It was at least eight feet wide and perhaps seven feet in length, and fitted with a modern mattress Ashley thought it would be superbly comfortable. Jake, who had been examining an oak chest which was standing against the wall in the same room, turned to find her stroking the scrollwork on one of the bedposts with a rather faraway look in her eyes. Walter Beswick was on his hands and knees beside the oak chest, trying to find any deterioration in the wood, and for a moment they were virtually alone.

'What are you thinking?' Jake asked, in her ear, and she started in surprise.

'Oh—it's you!' she exclaimed, aware that her heart was thumping unnecessarily loudly. 'I was just thinking—what a super bed this would make. Don't you think so?' She bent and pressed the yielding flock mattress that presently covered the solid base. 'With a decent mattress, of course.'

Jake folded his arms and studied the bed thoughtfully. 'Hmm. A bit cumbersome, don't you think? And much too big for one person.'

Ashley made a deprecating gesture. 'I wasn't meaning—for myself.'

'No?' Jake raised his dark eyebrows. 'For me, then? You think my fiancée would like something like this in our bedroom?'

Ashley bent her head, her enthusiasm for the piece fading. 'I was just speaking metaphorically,' she said.

'Metaphorically?' murmured Jake, in admiration. 'Now that's a very good word. What does it mean?'

Ashley opened her mouth to tell him and then closed it again at the mocking glint in his eyes. Turning away, she said determinedly: 'Where is the library? I'd like to see it.'

There was silence for a moment and she waited uneasily for him to reply. But when he did, it was something entirely different. 'If you'd like the bed, I'll buy it for you.'

Ashley swung round then, her eyes wide and alarmed. 'Oh, no! No, thank you.' Apart from the practicalities involved, she could just imagine the gossip if it ever emerged that Jake Seton had bought her a bed. Then she faltered, tipping her head on one side, trying to read his expression. Was she taking seriously again something that could only be a joke? 'You're not serious, are you?'

Jake's arms fell to his sides. 'Why not?'

Ashley shifted uneasily from one foot to the other. 'Well, because—where would I put a bed like that?' She tried to laugh, and failed abysmally.

'You'll be getting married one day. I've no doubt some arrangement could be made to store the bed until then——'

'No!' Ashley looked down at her hands, up at him and then down at her hands again. 'Thank you, but no.'

To her relief Walter Beswick came to join them then, marking something down in his catalogue. He was nodding in a satisfied way and Jake said: 'What do you think?'

'Oh, I think so—very definitely,' remarked Walter, patting Jake on the shoulders. 'Shall we go downstairs?'

The library was quite extensive, with a comprehensive collection of classical literature as well as many modern novels. Among the rarer volumes was a first folio of Shakespeare's plays, and a German Bible which Jake told Ashley was a common constituent among book collections. The most valued item was an illuminated manuscript illustrating one of the books of the New Testament, and this was kept apart from the others and no one was allowed to handle it.

But Ashley was quite content to browse through the rest of the books, and she was glad she was able to do so when a group of collectors finally annexed Jake and took him away to see some paintings which were stacked indiscriminately at the bottom of the staircase.

She glanced at her watch. There was a decidedly hollow feeling now in the region of her stomach, and she was not surprised to discover it was half past twelve. Jake had said the sale was due to start at noon, but obviously he had been mistaken. She sighed. Perhaps she should have asked her aunt to make them some sandwiches. It seemed apparent that they were not going to have time for any lunch.

The sale eventually began at one o'clock, starting with the smaller items and gradually progressing to the larger ones. A room had been cleared at the back of the house and chairs were provided for those who wanted to sit down. Ashley found herself with Walter Beswick, half a dozen other men separating her from Jake, and she sat rather dejectedly in one of the hard wooden chairs wishing she had the effrontery to push her way through to Jake's side. But he seemed absorbed, and she felt too young and inexperienced to act any differently.

All the small moveable items for auction were brought into the room, but Walter took the time to explain that the buyers were expected to examine the larger items before the sale and bid for them from the numbers in their catalogues.

There were quite a number of paintings, mostly portraits and landscapes, which even Ashley could see were practically worthless. But there was a picture by Gauguin which appealed to her very much, and she was not surprised to discover that Jake was interested in it, too. The bidding was brisk, but she was disappointed when Jake dropped out and another man bought it for what seemed like a reasonable sum. She wished she had been near enough to commiserate with Jake, but when next she caught a glimpse of him he didn't appear too concerned.

The library came next, and as expected the illuminated manuscript caused quite a stir. But afterwards, apart from one or two editions which were sold separately, the majority of the books were bought by a dealer from Leeds. Ashley felt quite sad at the thought that they were to be taken from their shelves where they had no doubt rested together for years and years to be sold independently over the counter in some secondhand bookshop.

The afternoon drew on. Ashley was feeling terribly hungry. She had only had a slice of toast and a cup of tea before leaving that morning, and apart from the cup of coffee they had bought at the top of Sutton Bank, nothing since. She should have made sure she had a good breakfast before leaving, but she had been too excited to eat much then.

As far as she could see, Jake hadn't bought a thing so far, and she wondered whether they were staying until the end. It was already three o'clock, and the windows were misty now, evidence of the chill air outside. There was still all the furniture to start on, and her spirits sank when she considered how long that might take. Surely none of these people had had any lunch. Didn't they need nourishment?

She uncrossed her legs and crossed them again, trying to stimulate her circulation. It wasn't cold in the room, but it wasn't warm either, and the continual sustainment of one position was apt to stiffen her limbs.

'Are you ready to go?'

She had been unaware that Jake had left his acquaintances and come to stand by her chair. She looked up at him uncomprehendingly. 'I thought you wanted to bid for the furniture,' she whispered, in surprise.

'Walter knows what I'm interested in,' replied Jake, in low tones. 'Don't you, Walter?'

Walter Beswick got to his feet. 'Of course. Are you leaving now?'

Jake nodded, flicking back his cuff and examining his watch. 'It's half past three. I don't want to be too late back.' He glanced meaningfully in Ashley's direction.

Walter nodded understandingly, but Ashley got to her feet rather indignantly. 'You don't have to leave on my account,' she declared.

Jake half smiled, his lean face disturbingly attractive. 'Don't I? That's good to know.'

He patted Walter's shoulder, and conveyed silent instructions, and Walter moved his head slowly up and down. 'I'll ring you tomorrow, Jake,' he said. 'About ten?'

'Fine.' Jake indicated that Ashley should precede him. 'I'll be seeing you.'

Walter smiled, his well-rounded face beaming. 'You will. G'bye. G'bye, Ashley.'

'Goodbye, Mr. Beswick.' Ashley tried to appear coolly composed, but didn't quite make it. She felt worse now than she had done at the start of their journey, and she was convinced that she was dragging Jake away from the sale at a time when he would have been most interested.

Outside, the cold air stung her cheeks, and she hurried across to the Ferrari, holding her coat collar closely about her throat. Jake unlocked the car doors and she quickly got inside, not even pausing to take off her coat as he did and throw it carelessly into the back. She sat hunched up in her seat, her knees together, her whole attitude emanating disapproval.

Jake closed his door and looked sideways at her. Then he sighed. 'Now what's wrong? You're a very transparent creature, Ashley. You don't make any attempt to hide your feelings, do you?'

Ashley tugged distractedly at the fingers of her suede gloves. 'You know perfectly well what's wrong,' she exclaimed. 'You've only left because of me. You said so.'

Jake shook his head. 'I've left, as you put it, because I've had enough. I wanted to leave. Do you mind? I'd have thought you'd be dying of hunger by now. Did you think I was going to starve you?'

Ashley made an involuntary gesture. 'But you haven't bought anything!'

'Haven't I?' His eyes narrowed. 'I'm not dissatisfied with the way things have gone, so why should you be?'

'Because if I wasn't here, you would stay!'

'Ashley, if you weren't here, I shouldn't have come,' he stated disconcertingly, and left her to ponder on that as he started the car and drove smoothly out of the stone gateway.

The light was fading when Jake eventually pulled off the road into the car park of a large, well-lit building, which looked rather like a country house. He had driven fast down the motorway and she had begun to think that he was hoping to reach Bewford in time for an evening meal. The pangs of hunger had been stilled by the motion of the car, and she had her thoughts to occupy her.

The engine was switched off and Jake said: 'Come on! I'm hungry. They do a damn good steak here.'

Ashley hesitated. 'But ought we to stop?' she questioned. 'I thought you were in a hurry to get home.'

Jake sighed, somewhat impatiently. 'You know, you're the most argumentative female I know,' he said, reaching for his coat. 'Why should you imagine I was in a hurry to get home? Did I say so?'

'No,' she admitted. 'But you drove fast down the motorway.'

'I always drive fast on motorways—and besides, I'm hungry. Aren't you?'

Ashley pressed her lips together, giving him a rather sheepish smile. 'Ravenous!'

Jake shook his head, and thrust open his door, and realising he was not about to comment, she did likewise.

Frost was already glinting on the ground in places, but fortunately it was dry and there was little danger of the roads becoming icy. They walked across to the lighted entrance of the building, and as they walked, Jake explained:

'This used to be a manor house, about twenty years ago. The chap who owns it went to school with my father. Unfortunately, his family ran into financial difficulties and money was pretty tight, and that was when Paul—that's this fellow's name—had this brilliant idea of turning the place into a sort of country club. They owned the land adjoining it, so now they provide golf and tennis, and swimming in the season.'

Ashley was intrigued, but when he had finished speaking, she ventured: 'But won't this man—this friend of your father's—think it odd? I mean—you coming here with someone other than your fiancée?'

They had reached the entrance and Jake took her arm and pushed her rather roughly ahead of him into the building. Ashley was surprised, but when she looked round she

46

saw his face was grim. However, he didn't say anything right then, but took off his coat and handed it to the receptionist standing in a cubicle by the door. Ashley hesitated and then she, too, took off her coat and did likewise.

'The cloakrooms are through there,' he remarked, indicating an alcove to their right. 'Shall I wait?'

Ashley was about to say that she didn't need to use the cloakroom when a feeling that perhaps her nose was shining with the cold occurred to her. 'All right,' she agreed, in a small voice, and walked away with as much elegance as she could muster.

At this hour of the evening, the cloakroom was deserted. It was very attractive and luxurious, with pink and gold fitments and lots of long mirrors. Ashley regarded her reflection without enjoyment, critically examining her cream slacks for creases which ought not to be there. The red blouse looked reasonably crisp, but she wished she had chosen to wear a pendant of some sort. She seldom wore jewellery, and she thought her throat looked a little bare for dining out.

Her nose, thankfully, was not shining, but she smoothed some cleansing tissues over her skin and applied a light foundation. Her lipstick was almost the same colour as her hair when it glinted in the artificial lights, and her long lashes required no further darkening. She tugged a comb through the tangled thickness of her hair and had to be satisfied with the end result. She thought she didn't look too bad considering she had been out all day.

A hollow little rumble in her stomach reminded her that she had still had nothing to eat, and gripping her bag tightly, she left the cloakroom and went in search of Jake. He was still standing where she had left him, but he was no longer alone. Two people were talking with him, a middle-aged man and woman, and judging from their appearance, Ashley guessed that they were probably the owners of the place.

She crossed the soft carpet of the hall almost silently, but when Jake saw her coming he half turned and said: 'Here's Ashley now.' Then, to her alone: 'All right?'

Ashley nodded, trying to appear cool and sophisticated.

These people were friends of Jake's family and she didn't want to let him down by behaving childishly. 'Thank you, yes,' she answered, looking at the others. 'I was sure my nose was shining. You know how it is when one has been out all day. One feels an absolute hag!'

She sensed rather than saw Jake stiffen beside her. In fact, she was avoiding looking directly at him, and she was relieved when the woman smiled understandingly. She was rather an attractive woman, slim and elegant, with immaculately styled blue-grey hair, and a youthfully unlined face. 'Yes, I know, my dear,' she exclaimed. 'And it's been so cold, hasn't it? I expect you're simply dying for a drink —something strong and warming!'

Ashley's shaky bubble of confidence exploded. 'Well— yes,' she murmured awkwardly, realising belatedly that they were bound to imagine she was over eighteen. Her eyes went appealingly to Jake, but now he chose not to acknowledge it.

'As you've probably guessed, this is Grace and Paul Freeman, Ashley,' he said. Then, to the others: 'I was telling her about your success with this place on our way here.'

'Hello, Ashley.' Paul Freeman's hand was reassuringly firm. He was a big man, as tall as Jake but much broader, with muscular shoulders which would not have looked out of place on a wrestler. 'I hear you've been to a sale at Raybury.'

'Yes.' Ashley strove to appear composed. 'It was very interesting—although I didn't buy anything.'

By general consent they all began to move towards the cocktail bar, and as they walked Ashley found Grace by her side.

'Have you known Jake long?' she asked, and Ashley couldn't be sure whether the question was loaded or not.

'No, not long,' she conceded. 'I haven't lived in Bewford very long. My—my father died a few months ago, and now I live with my uncle and aunt.'

'I see,' Grace nodded slowly. 'You know Barbara, of course.'

'Barbara?' Ashley played for time. 'You mean—Jake's fiancée?' She shook her head. 'Not personally—no.'

Grace's narrow brows ascended. 'No?' She glanced round at Jake talking quietly to her husband behind them. 'I thought you did.' She folded her hands. 'She's my niece, you see.'

Ashley was astounded. 'Is she?' she murmured faintly. 'How nice. I—they're getting married soon, aren't they?'

'Yes. In June.' Grace looked more relaxed as she spoke. 'It will be a lovely wedding. They're such a handsome couple, don't you think?'

As Ashley had never even seen Barbara, she could hardly judge. But she was sensible enough not to volunteer that kind of information, and merely smiled as though the question was purely rhetorical.

As they entered the cocktail bar, a waitress appeared with some query about the evening's menus, and Grace excused herself to go and attend to it. Ashley was somewhat relieved at her departure, but when Paul Freeman himself went behind the bar to mix their drinks, dismissing the bartender's services, she was forced to cast an appealing look in Jake's direction. Surely he was going to say something. After all, apart from anything else, she wasn't accustomed to alcohol.

But Jake was aloof, his eyes barely registering her presence as he indicated that she should take one of the tall stools beside the bar. Ashley hesitated only a moment and then gritting her teeth she perched on the circular leather seat. If that was the way he wanted to play it, then she wouldn't disappoint him, she decided defiantly.

A frosted glass of some tawny liquid was set in front of her, chinking with ice, and Paul stood before her saying: 'Try that. It's a speciality of the house.'

Ashley took one final look at Jake before complying, but he was lighting a cheroot with lazily controlled movements and showed not the slightest interest in her plight.

With a sinking heart she raised the glass to her lips and swallowed a mouthful. Its sharpness caught the back of her throat and she had to cough to relieve the choking sensation it evoked. Putting down the glass she looked up into Paul's expectant face.

'Well?' he said. 'What did you think?'

'Oh—oh, it's lovely,' she lied, her vocal chords shredded and needing clearing again. 'What is it?'

'Ah, that would be telling,' smiled Paul with obvious satisfaction. Then to Jake: 'What'll it be? Mother's ruin or a drop of the hard stuff?'

Jake seemed to find something in Paul's face rather amusing, and he had difficulty in articulating. But at last he said: 'Scotch would be fine. But not a large one. I'm driving. I have to limit my alcoholic intake—haven't I, Ashley?' and he gave her a sidelong stare.

Ashley was furious. He was deliberately making fun of her. He knew she wasn't old enough to drink alcohol in hotels and country clubs. What was he expecting her to do? Own up to Paul Freeman? Admit that she was a minor? Her fingers tightened round her glass again. Well, she wouldn't do it. She would play him at his own game. After all, she would be eighteen in a few weeks, and the sooner she learnt how to take wines and spirits, the better.

She swallowed another mouthful of the liquid in her glass. It was horrible, but at least this time it didn't make her cough quite so much. Maybe if she had a cigarette that would soothe her throat. It felt quite raw at the moment.

'May I have a cigarette?' she enquired, of neither one of them.

Jake's eyes swung in her direction. 'I didn't know you smoked.'

'But then you don't know everything about me, do you?' she countered.

Paul drew a case out of his pocket. 'Have one of mine,' he offered. 'They're Turkish, I'm afraid, but I like them.'

Determinedly stiffening her resolve Ashley took one of the gold-tipped cigarettes and put it between her lips. Jake flicked his lighter and held it out and she leant towards him, steadying his hand with her own. His skin was cool and firm, reassuringly steady in a world that as she drew on the cigarette became decidedly unsteady. Her startled eyes registered annoyance in his, but she had little resilience at that moment to challenge him. Instead she drew back, gripping the bar with one hand and wishing she had not started this ridiculous charade. Obviously the alcohol she had consumed on an empty stomach was responsible for her giddiness, and the Turkish cigarette made her feel sick.

She slid off the stool abruptly. 'Excuse me!' she managed, and ignoring Jake's: 'Where are you going?' she hurried unsteadily across the bar, out through the arched entrance, and over the seemingly vast expanse of hall carpet to where the sign *Ladies' Cloakroom* offered a blessed haven.

Once inside, in its pink and gold luxury, she sought an ashtray and got rid of the strong Turkish cigarette before resting her forehead weakly against the cool tiles that provided a splashback for the washbasins. Although she still felt sick, she was empty inside, and as the dizziness subsided only nausea remained.

What a fool she had made of herself, she thought miserably, and all because Jake had been angry at her suggestion that these people might find their relationship strange. What she had half accepted before was impressed more firmly upon her now—Jake regarded her as he would regard the cousin of any of his friends—with indulgence and kindness and friendly interest. She was to blame for reading more into his motives than he had intended, for trying to behave like a woman of the world. That was the last thing she could claim. In fact, by behaving as she had, she had reduced her real age by several years.

A sudden knocking at the cloakroom door brought her upright and trembling, hastily taking a look at her reflection, conscious of being unprepared to face anyone right now.

'Ashley! Ashley, are you in there?'

It was Jake's voice, and Ashley's lips parted. 'Y-yes, I'm here,' she stammered. 'I—I won't be long.'

'I want you to come out now,' stated Jake grimly. 'At once.'

'I—I can't. I'm—I'm doing my hair——'

'*Now*, Ashley!'

'No——'

She was completely unprepared for what happened next. The door swung open and he stood in the aperture, glaring at her. His gaze raked her tear-filled eyes, her pale cheeks and trembling mouth, the way her fingers tugged revealingly at the strap of her bag.

'I knew it!' he exclaimed harshly. 'You're hiding away in here like a frightened mouse! What in God's name were you planning to do? Run away?'

CHAPTER FOUR

ASHLEY moved her shoulders in a jerky fashion. 'Of course not,' she denied. 'I—I—do I have to give you my reasons for using the cloakroom? I should have thought they—were private.'

'Rubbish!' His tone was flat. 'You dived in here like a fox down its hole. And why? To powder your nose? I don't think so.'

Ashley bent her head. 'If you must know, I felt sick——'

'I'm not surprised.'

'Of course. You wouldn't be, would you?' she demanded then, anger inspiring a little courage inside her.

'What's that supposed to mean?'

'You *know*!'

'Do I?' He was deliberately obtuse.

Ashley looked down at her feet again. 'Why didn't you tell—Mr. Freeman—that I was under eighteen?'

'Why didn't you?'

Ashley shrugged. 'How could I?'

'After the way you acted? I agree.'

'What do you mean—after the way I acted?' Ashley stared at him.

'Are you going to deny you tried to behave like—well, like someone you're not?'

'I didn't want to embarrass you, that's all,' she declared stiffly. 'Taking out a schoolgirl!'

'If I choose to take out schoolgirls, that's my affair.'

'Mrs. Freeman is your fiancée's aunt.'

'I know that.'

Ashley stared at him tremulously and then looked away. 'We—we can't stand here talking——'

'We appear to be managing quite successfully,' he remarked, folding his arms.

'That's not what I meant, and you know it,' Ashley sighed.

'Then come out of there,' he advised, standing aside so that she could do so.

Ashley hesitated only a moment and then with uneasy steps she did as he asked, and the door swung closed behind her. Fortunately no one appeared to have noticed what had been going on, or perhaps the Freemans had made sure no one noticed, thought Ashley, with unusual cynicism. But right now she was feeling utterly depressed.

'Now,' he said, taking her upper arm firmly between his fingers, 'I suggest we go and do what we intended to do when we arrived here.'

Ashley's eyes were startled. 'What's that?'

'Eat!' he stated briefly.

'I—I don't think I could eat anything——'

'Don't be silly.' His tone was that of a parent reproving a child. 'You only feel sick because you're empty inside.'

'That drink I had made me feel sick,' she accused hotly.

'Are you sure it wasn't the cigarette?' His tone was mild. 'I've never heard of anyone becoming intoxicated on ginger cordial and soda water!'

Ashley halted abruptly, looking at him disbelievingly. 'You mean, that was—that was all it was?'

Jake's expression was lazily indulgent. 'Now you didn't think I would allow Paul to risk his licence by serving alcohol to a minor, did you?'

'Then—you told him how old I was?'

Jake nodded.

'But why did you let me go on believing that you hadn't?'

Jake's lips twisted. 'I didn't want to spoil your performance. And it was quite a performance, wasn't it?'

'Why, you—you——' Ashley wrenched her arm out of his grasp. 'What a rotten thing to do!'

'Well, you were the one who was concerned about my reputation, weren't you?' he reminded her. 'Would you have had the Freemans think you were—I don't know— something else, maybe?'

'What sort of something else?'

Jake looked down into her puzzled face. 'Would you believe—my mistress?'

. Ashley's face flamed. He had put into words something which hitherto even she had been loath to contemplate. Perhaps because some insidious demon inside her welcomed the wanton connotation.

She fought to banish such thoughts. 'You can't be serious?' she protested.

'Why not?' He flexed his back muscles wearily. 'You assuredly don't look like any schoolgirl in that gear.'

His gaze shifted away from her and Ashley drew a deep breath. *How do I look, then?* she wanted to ask, but had not the courage to voice it. Instead, Jake seemed to take this as an end to the conversation and indicated that she should precede him into the restaurant.

There were one or two other diners even at this early hour, but they were shown to a table near the long windows. A centrepiece of miniature daffodils and crocuses was illuminated by a single thick red candle, and combined with the concealed lighting above the moulding near the ceiling gave the place a rather intimate air.

A white-coated attendant came to take their order and Ashley studied the huge menu she had been handed without really seeing it. She started when Jake spoke to her, but nodded at his suggestion of steak and french fries with a prawn cocktail to begin with.

The meal was delicious, as Ashley had known it would be. The prawns were thick and juicy, and the steak was grilled exactly as she liked it. Although she began by being sure she would be able to eat none of it, her naturally healthy appetite was revived by the dry white wine that Jake had ordered and she found herself eating enthusiastically, not replete until the last morsel of raspberry gateau had been consumed.

As they ate she asked him rather tentatively about the auction. It, at least, was a safe subject, and she was fascinated by his knowledge of antiques and their origins, though she was surprised by it.

'That Gauguin painting,' she ventured, toying with her wine glass. 'I thought you gave up too easily.'

Jake half smiled. 'Really?'

'Yes. Oh, I don't know a lot about painting, of course,

but I thought the price it was sold for was very reasonable, didn't you?'

Jake nodded. 'Very reasonable,' he agreed.

'So why didn't you buy it, then? I mean, you could have gone a little higher, couldn't you?' She flushed. She was getting out of her depth again. Jake's finances were nothing to do with her.

But he didn't seem to mind. 'The painting is mine,' he stated quietly. 'Or at least it will be by the end of the day.'

'What do you mean?' She was confused, her green eyes wide and unknowingly appealing.

'Auctions are not always what they seem, Ashley. Haven't you heard of arrangements being made between dealers? Of private auctions after the public one?'

Ashley frowned. 'Vaguely.' She paused. 'But is that legal?'

Jake shrugged. 'It's expedient. Why should we bid highly for something which between ourselves we could sell for a much less exorbitant price?'

'Yes. But you're not a dealer, are you?'

'No. But Walter is.'

'I see.' Ashley traced her nail round the rim of her glass. 'I must seem very stupid.'

Jake made no reply to this, but his eyes were lazily mocking as he began talking about his travels abroad, changing the subject entirely. He was an interesting raconteur. She had not realised how widely he had travelled and she found herself questioning him about the places he had visited, fascinated by his knowledge of cultures and customs. In no time at all it seemed they were drinking their coffee at the end of the meal, Jake taking his strong and black with a balloon glass of cognac to accompany it.

He glanced at his watch as Ashley refused a second cup of coffee, and said rather dryly: 'Are you aware that it's after seven?'

Ashley looked at her own watch. 'Goodness! So it is.' She smiled. 'The time has flown.'

'I'll take that as a compliment,' he remarked lazily, rising to his feet. 'But I really think we must go. Your aunt and uncle will be getting quite anxious about you, I think.'

Ashley stood up reluctantly. He was right, of course. Her aunt and uncle would be getting concerned about her, but there was an awful dejected feeling in the pit of her stomach when she considered that in a little over half an hour their day would be over.

The Freemans were in the hall as they left, talking to a group of new arrivals, but Paul turned when he saw them and said: 'Enjoy your meal, Ashley?'

Ashley nodded, rather shamefaced. 'Very much.'

'I hope we didn't upset you too much earlier on,' added Paul gently. 'It was only funning.'

She shook her head and went to get her coat when a woman's voice hailed Jake. 'Jake! Jake Seton! Fancy seeing you here! Where's Barbara?'

Ashley was conscious of an intense feeling of embarrassment as a small dark girl in a red trouser suit and a fur jacket caught his arm. But Jake seemed quite at ease. 'Hello, Angela,' he greeted her casually. 'I didn't know you knew this place.'

'Of course I know it. I've been here with Babs.' Angela frowned and looked all round. 'Where is she? She is with you, isn't she?'

'No.' Jake took his sheepskin coat from the receptionist and proceeded to put it on. 'Angela, I'd like you to meet Ashley Calder. Ashley, this is a friend of Barbara's—Angela Thorne.'

'How do you do, Miss Thorne?' Ashley shook hands reluctantly.

'Hello.' Angela Thorne regarded her unsmilingly. Then to Jake: 'I don't remember Barbara ever mentioning anyone by that name—Ashley. It's most unusual, isn't it?'

'It is rather,' Jake smiled. 'Well, don't let us keep you from your friends. We're just leaving. Ready, Ashley?'

Ashley nodded, conscious of the other girl's appraising stare, but with another casual word of farewell, Jake was urging her ahead of him and they emerged from the warmth of the hall into the freezing night air.

The Ferrari was cold, but the engine fired instantly, and Jake drove smoothly out of the car park. He had not taken off his coat this time, and Ashley huddled inside hers wondering whether that last encounter had really meant as little to him as he pretended.

When a couple of miles separated them from the country club, he said: 'Why do you let people upset you? Angela Thorne means nothing to me.'

'She'll tell your fiancée that she's seen you—with me!'

'So?' Jake sighed. 'Ashley, I fully intend to tell Barbara myself.'

'Oh, I see.' Ashley turned her head to stare out of the side window. She was being foolish again. Of course he would tell his fiancée. And why not? It had been a perfectly innocent expedition.

All too soon it seemed the lights of Bewford were visible below them and Jake accelerated along Grange Road before turning into the High Street and bringing the Ferrari to a searing halt outside the Golden Lion.

Ashley reached for the door catch, but before she could open it, Jake had stretched across her and prevented her from doing so. His arm was hard against her yielding body, as it had been once before, and Ashley felt a devastating surge of emotion at his nearness. She could have sworn the pressure was increased deliberately for a moment, and then he flung himself back in his seat, a grim expression marring his lean features. Looking down at his hands curved about the bottom of the steering wheel, he said:

'Thank you for coming. Goodnight.'

Ashley was all weak and breathless. 'G-goodnight,' she stammered, fumbling with the door catch. 'And—and thank you. I—I have enjoyed it.'

'Good.' He looked up then and although he obviously had himself in control there was something in the depths of his eyes which quickened Ashley's movements and sent her hurrying out of the car.

She turned on the pavement and slammed the door, and without another word the Ferrari surged away, its taillights illuminating the High Street until it disappeared round a bend in the road. Only then did Ashley move to enter the hotel, her whole system a churning mass of repressed emotions.

Her aunt was in the dining room when Ashley entered the building, but she heard the sound of the door closing and came to see who was there.

'Oh, Ashley!' she exclaimed, her plump face beaming with relief. 'I was getting so worried about you!'

Ashley forced a smile. 'Why? You knew it was a long way to Raybury.' She kissed her aunt's cheek. 'But thank you anyway, for caring.'

Mona gave her a quick hug. 'I was just clearing the table. I left your meal in the oven and the table set in case you were hungry when you got home—oh! Has Jake gone straight home?'

'Why, yes,' Ashley nodded.

'Thank goodness for that.' Mona led the way into the kitchen. 'I've had his mother on the phone twice asking if I knew where he was.'

'His mother?' Ashley was astonished. 'But why?'

Mona bent to take a dish out of the oven. 'Well, apparently they're having some sort of dinner party this evening and Jake was expected to be there.'

'I see.' Ashley found it difficult to swallow. 'So—so what did you say?'

'Well, I told her as much as I knew. That you'd gone to Raybury and I didn't know what time you'd be back. I said I didn't think you'd be late, though.' Mona placed the dish of tuna pie on the kitchen table. 'It won't take a minute to heat the sauce. Are you hungry?'

Ashley sighed. 'Not at all, I'm afraid. We—we had dinner on our way back.'

'Dinner!' Her aunt was astonished. 'But what about Jake's mother's dinner party?'

Ashley nodded uncomfortably. 'I know. But I knew nothing about it.'

Mona shook her head. 'Oh, well, it's none of my business.' She looked regretfully at the pie. 'I suppose this might heat up for our lunch tomorrow.' She grimaced, and then looked back at Ashley. 'So—how did you enjoy yourself?'

'Very much.' Ashley undid the leather fastenings on her coat. 'It was very interesting. It was a terribly old building with lots of ghastly Victorian furniture. But there were some good pieces—antiques, I suppose. And there were lots of people there.' She was forcing herself to an enthusiasm that was hard to make convincing in her state of mind. But fortunately her aunt was too concerned with Jake's misdemeanours and the fate of the tuna pie to ask too many difficult questions.

The difficulties came later that night when Karen came home, bright-eyed and eager to know what happened.

'I told Rita Ferris that you had gone to Raybury with Jake Seton and she didn't believe me!' she declared resentfully. 'Just wait until she finds out from someone else! She'll be green with envy!' She perched confidingly on the side of Ashley's bed. 'Well? What happened?'

Ashley sighed. 'Nothing much. We went to the sale. We spent—oh, I don't know—perhaps four hours there, and then we came home. Oh—and we had dinner at some country club on the way.'

'Nothing much!' echoed Karen. 'You call that nothing much! Gosh, even going out in the Ferrari would satisfy me! You lucky cat! What did he say to you? What did you talk about? Did he make a pass at you?'

'Of course not.' Ashley was hot and embarrassed now. 'He—he's not like that.'

'All men are like that,' replied Karen, with worldly cynicism. 'They all want what they can't have.'

'You're not suggesting that Jake Seton wants me, are you?' demanded Ashley, propping herself up on her elbows.

Karen gave this some thought. 'I can't make up my mind,' she confessed.

'Well, I can make it up for you! He knew I was interested in books—in getting a job at the library. He thought I'd like to see a private library—and that's all!'

Karen looked at her askance. 'Oh, really? And do you think if he knew a post office was coming up for sale, he'd take me to see that?'

'Karen, you're just being silly. That's not the same.'

'No, perhaps not.' Karen got up from the bed and began to take off her clothes. 'All the same, you have to admit, he does seem to enjoy your company, doesn't he?'

Ashley flopped back on her pillows. 'I—I don't know.'

Karen pulled a wry face. 'Of course you do. What I'm wondering is—what will his next excuse be?'

'What do you mean?'

'Well, he gave you a lift home from school, didn't he? And he came into the bar to see you——'

'He didn't know I was in the bar!' Ashley was indignant. 'He knows I'm not allowed to serve in the bar!'

'All right.' Karen tipped her head on one side. 'Perhaps that was accidental. But who's to say he wouldn't have come round and asked you anyway?'

'You're making mountains out of molehills,' said Ashley crossly, pulling the bedcovers up to her chin. 'He's probably bored, that's all.'

.'Bored?' Karen fastened the buttons of her pyjama jacket. 'Why should he be bored? He has plenty of things to do.'

Ashley looked reluctantly over the blankets. 'Like what?'

Karen sniffed. 'Are you really interested? I thought the subject was beginning to bore you.'

Ashley gave an exasperated sigh. 'Don't be so mean!' she cried. 'What does he do with his time?'

'He's the chairman of the company, of course.'

'Company? What company?' Ashley was confused.

'The Seton company, of course.' Karen was impatient. 'You surely didn't imagine Jake could run a Ferrari on the profits from the estate, did you?'

Ashley propped herself up again. 'What sort of business is he in?'

Karen sank down on to the side of her bed. 'Banking, property—that sort of thing. I've heard Daddy say that the Setons own most of Bewford, one way and another.'

'I had no idea.' Ashley lay back on her pillows, a frown drawing her dark brows together. She was remembering her conversation with Jake that morning when she had made those ridiculous comments about him not having a career. What must he have thought of her?

Karen turned back her bedcovers. 'No, well, I don't suppose he would mention it,' she remarked, climbing between the sheets. 'I've heard that he never wanted to join the company, but his father insisted. He's the only son, you see.'

Now Ashley was interested, and Karen was closing her eyes. 'Don't go to sleep,' she exclaimed, leaning across the space between their beds to tug Karen's covers. 'Just tell me—what did he want to do?'

Karen opened her eyes and from the mischief gleaming in their depths, Ashley guessed that she had closed them deliberately. 'Why do you want to know?' she asked, with irritating innocence.

Ashley heaved a sigh. 'Does it matter? I'm curious, that's all.'

Karen yawned. 'It's late and I'm tired.'

Ashley's face mirrored her disappointment and her cousin relented.

'Oh, all right,' she said. 'He went to Cambridge and got a degree in languages. He wanted to be an interpreter.'

'I see.'

Ashley lay back again. It fitted, of course. His interest in other countries—the amount of travelling he had done—his intimate knowledge of development and intellect overseas. But his father had wanted him to follow in his footsteps.

Karen turned on her side. 'Ashley,' she said quietly.

'Yes?' Ashley looked at her.

'I don't quite know how to say this, but—well, be careful, won't you?'

Ashley looked away. 'I don't know what you mean.'

'Yes, you do. Ash, Jake Seton is a lot older than you are, a lot less vulnerable than you are, and a whole hell of a lot more experienced than you are. Don't—get involved with him.'

Ashley tried to appear amused. 'You're taking it all much too seriously, Karen. I've told you——'

'I know what you've told me,' said Karen, turning on to her back. 'Oh, well, don't say I didn't warn you!'

She reached for the switch on her bedside lamp and the room was plunged into darkness. Within minutes, Ashley heard her cousin's steady breathing, but she was far from sleep. Although she was tired her brain simply refused to stop functioning. The events of the day were too sharply etched upon her thoughts to allow her to relax in sleep.

What had happened when Jake finally arrived home? Had his mother been really angry? And if so, what had been his reaction? Remembering the way he had dismissed unfavourable reactions to their outing, she couldn't help wondering whether he had deliberately delayed his return to frustrate his parents. But why? For what purpose? And why make her a party to it?

She rolled on to her stomach and bunched up her pillows, burying her head in them. She must stop thinking about him. Today had been a day out of time. It was hardly likely to be repeated, and the sooner she accepted that the better.

CHAPTER FIVE

DURING the following week, the weather got considerably warmer, and the scent of spring was in the air. Trees and bushes started burgeoning with new life, and daffodils grew everywhere. There were lambs in the fields, free now from the grip of snow and ice, and Mark said that one of his mares had foaled. He offered to take Ashley up to see it, but she politely declined, making some excuse about having a headache, and he didn't ask her again. She guessed that he had decided she was only making excuses, but she hoped he didn't suspect why. But the idea of going up to the hall, of risking seeing Jake again, was best avoided.

Then, the following weekend, there was a horse show at Hislop. Some of the Setons' horses were taking part, and Mona suggested that Ashley might like to go with Mark.

Ashley couldn't refuse. The last time she had gone out with Mark she had enjoyed herself so much that to refuse would have hurt his feelings terribly. So she pretended an enthusiasm she didn't really feel, and told herself that there was absolutely no chance of seeing Jake that day.

And, in fact, Jake was not at the show. But instead of feeling relieved, Ashley only felt disappointment, and inwardly chided herself for being so stupid.

Afterwards she drove home with Mark in one of the estate station wagons, towing a horsebox behind them. They drove straight to the stables, and Ashley stood about impatiently, her hands thrust into the pockets of her navy duffel coat, waiting for Mark and the stable boys to finish grooming the animals. She saw Mark coming towards her when the sound of horses' hooves sounded in the lane outside, and a moment later Jake Seton and a woman Ashley did not recognise, but whom she could guess the identity of, rode into the stable yard.

Jake looked good on a horse, the tight-fitting breeches accentuating the muscular strength of his legs as he swung himself to the ground. His companion seemed equally capable, controlling her animal with assured confidence when it protested at the sudden curtailment of its freedom.

Jake patted his horse's neck, and with a casual glance towards the woman who had ridden with him, he walked over to where Mark and Ashley were standing.

'Hello,' he said, his greeting encompassing both of them. 'Had a good day?'

'Reasonably good,' replied Mark. 'Prince developed a limp and had to be withdrawn from the point-to-point, but the Lass and Manitoba did quite well.'

Jake frowned, concerned for the moment with his horse. 'What do you think is wrong with Prince? Nothing serious, I hope.'

'Oh, no. Pulled tendons, I think,' Mark assured him. 'Your mother rode him to hounds last week and I think it happened then.'

'Ah!' Jake nodded understandingly, and then his gaze shifted to Ashley. 'And did you enjoy it?'

Ashley's mouth felt stiff. 'Yes, thank you,' she answered politely. Like a child having just enjoyed an unexpected treat, she thought frustratedly, aware of the limitations of jeans and a duffel coat when compared to the expensively styled jodhpurs and mohair jacket that his companion was wearing. The other woman had left her horse in the charge of one of the stable hands and had approached them while Jake was talking, and when her hand touched his arm he swung round, his lips twisting strangely.

'You haven't met Mark's cousin Ashley, have you, Barbara?'

Barbara St. John Forrest shook her head. She was of medium height, but her slender build made her appear smaller, and Ashley thought she had never seen anyone more attractive. Her hair was short and silky, shaping her head like a silver cap, while arched brows ascended over dark eyes and high cheekbones. Her mouth was red and rather full, perhaps her least attractive feature, but there was sensuality there and a certain wilfulness, too.

'Hello, Ashley,' she said, assessing the younger girl without enthusiasm. 'I have heard Jake mention you.'

'How do you do?' The words stuck in Ashley's throat, but she forced herself to be polite, conscious of Jake's eyes upon her.

Barbara turned to Mark and smiled. Clearly the opposite sex was of more interest to her. 'Have you had a good day?'

Mark responded with what Ashley considered was an unnecessary show of deference, and she moved her feet restlessly, wishing they had got away before the others returned.

'We've been across to High Ingram,' Barbara was saying to Mark. 'I expect you know the Messiters.' She sighed. 'We were invited to lunch with them, and after so much fresh air I'm feeling positively exhausted, aren't you, darling?' She turned her attention to her fiancé.

Jake shrugged, his hands deep in the pockets of his breeches. 'Perhaps I'm more used to exercise than you are,' he remarked mockingly, and she gave him a playful punch, entirely for their benefit, Ashley decided with unaccustomed bitchiness. But quite honestly, the day had gone sour on her and she longed to get away from Jake and his fiancée.

She gave Mark a pointed look and he took the hint. 'We must be going,' he said. 'I'm sure Ashley's starving, aren't you, love?'

The endearment was appreciated and Ashley managed a faint smile. 'I am rather,' she admitted, although she doubted very much whether she would be able to eat much after this.

Jake looked down at Barbara, and then said: 'We're at a loose end this evening. Why don't you and your cousin come out for dinner with us, Mark?'

Ashley was horrified, but no more so than Barbara St. John Forrest. It was evident in the way her brows suddenly drew together, and the startled look she cast in Jake's direction. But he was not looking at her now, he was looking at Ashley, and she prayed that she would not show exactly how embarrassed she was.

However, Mark was apparently unaware of the undercurrents behind that seemingly innocent invitation, and after a moment's consideration said: 'That sounds rather tempting, Jake. Are you sure your fiancée doesn't mind?'

Jake barely glanced at Barbara. 'We'd be delighted if you could join us.'

'Well——' Mark looked doubtfully at Ashley, 'would you like to do that?'

Ashley thought there was nothing she would like less, but found it difficult to put into words. 'I—I've got nothing to wear,' she protested uncomfortably. 'It's very kind of you, but——'

'I'm sure you've got something suitable,' commented Jake, and she sensed the reproof behind his statement. 'We won't be going anywhere formal.'

Mark was keen, Ashley knew that, and realised that he saw nothing unusual in the invitation. After all, he and Jake were friends, they had been friends for a number of years, and now that he had someone to take out with him he was quite eager to enjoy Jake's company.

With a sigh, she acquiesced, aware as she did so that Barbara was not going to like it. She had actually said nothing, but if Jake was conscious of her silent disapproval, he chose to ignore it.

'Right,' said Jake now, stretching with disturbing, animal-like grace. 'I suggest we pick you up about seven—at the Golden Lion, of course.'

'Fine.' Mark nodded, looking at his watch. 'That gives us a couple of hours to make ourselves decent.' He grinned. 'Perhaps we'll be able to return the compliment in a couple of weeks when it's Ashley's birthday, hmm?'

Jake frowned. 'In two weeks?' He shook his head. 'You'll be eighteen in two weeks, Ashley?'

'Yes.' She half turned away, unable to sustain the probing penetration of his stare. 'Oughtn't we to be going, Mark?'

'Of course.' Mark collected his thoughts. 'I'll just make sure Simon knows I'm leaving. He can lock up.'

He walked away, and Ashley felt bereft of all support. Barbara was eyeing her with what Ashley felt sure was active dislike, but she couldn't be blamed for the situation. If Barbara had any complaints to make, she should make them to her fiancé.

The silence between the three of them became loaded with tension, and Jake broke it by saying: 'You'll be leaving school in three weeks, won't you? Have you had an interview at the library yet?'

Ashley shook her head. 'Not yet, no. I have an appointment for next Wednesday, actually.'

Jake listened with interest. He had the knack of directing his whole attention towards you so that you felt he was completely involved with what you were saying. 'And if you get the job—what then?'

Ashley licked her dry lips. 'Oh—oh, then I'd probably start work the week after Easter.'

Jake looked determinedly at his fiancée. 'Did you hear that? Ashley expects to start work in the County Library after Easter. When your library books need changing, you can have her do it for you.'

Barbara gave him an impatient look. 'I don't borrow library books,' she declared sharply. 'I don't have time for reading!'

'Then perhaps you should make time,' observed Jake dryly, and as though sensing that she had annoyed him Barbara was immediately contrite. It made Ashley feel rather sick watching her stroking his wrist in a deliberately intimate way, looking up at him seductively. She was inordinately relieved when Mark reappeared and said: 'Okay, everything's organised. Shall we go? See you later, Jake—Barbara!'

Mona and David Sutton were rather pleased that Jake had invited Mark and Ashley out for the evening. Ashley speculated that her aunt considered this latest move a confirmation that his apparent interest in her was without ulterior motivation, but Karen clearly had reservations. When Ashley was in their bedroom, getting ready to go out later, Karen entered the room unsmilingly and flung herself on her bed.

'Well!' she said challengingly. 'What did I tell you?'

Ashley turned from applying eye-shadow to her lids. 'What about?' she asked, assuming ignorance.

Karen swung into an upright position, her knees drawn

under her chin. 'You *know*!' she stated, staring at her cousin.

Ashley put down the brush she had been using and reached for her lipstick. 'I don't.' She frowned. 'Do you think this orange colour suits me? I just got it the other day——'

'I told you Jake would find another way of seeing you,' declared Karen abruptly. 'And I was right.'

Ashley sighed. 'You can't be serious. Heavens, Karen, his invitation was for Mark's benefit, not mine. And besides, why would he want to see me when he has Barbara St. John Forrest? From the look of her I should think she's more than capable of filling his needs!'

Karen smiled then, albeit unwillingly. 'That was an unusually catty thing for you to say.'

Ashley flushed. 'Well!' She moved her shoulders in a confused gesture. 'You know I'm right. You've seen her, haven't you?'

'Oh, yes, I know Barbara St. John Forrest. Her family have lived around here almost as long as the Setons.'

'There you are, then——'

'You can't honestly compare yourself to her!' exclaimed Karen, hotly. 'Good lord, that white hair is so synthetic! And she's old—at least twenty-five or six.'

'Ancient,' agreed Ashley dryly. 'Honestly, Karen, you're talking drivel! I couldn't begin to match her sophistication, and she knows it!'

'Perhaps Jake's a little bored with sophisticated women,' commented Karen, examining a snag in her tights. 'He's known plenty.'

'Karen, will you please stop saying things like that!' Ashley appealed to her. 'It's bad enough having to spend several hours in their company without having this kind of inquisition beforehand. I don't want to go, but what can I do? Pretend to be ill? Say I've got a headache?'

'Oh, no, you'll have to go.' Karen was laconic. 'But for goodness' sake, see it the way it is! Not the way you'd like it to be.'

Irritably Ashley swept open the wardrobe door. 'So what do you suggest I wear? Sackcloth and ashes?'

'It would look better on you than on her!' retorted Karen, studying her cousin critically. 'You know now that Mum's cooking is putting some flesh on your bones, you're getting quite a figure.' She sighed. 'I wish I was taller and slimmer. And I bet Barbara Forrest does, too.'

Ashley ignored her and riffled through her clothes. What could she wear? Trousers figured strongest among her things next to her school clothes, but none of them were suitable for dining out really. Karen slid off the bed and joined her, her head tipped on one side.

'What you want to wear is that blouse with the full sleeves—the green one—and a long skirt,' she said.

'I don't have a long skirt,' said Ashley impatiently. 'I've never had any use for one before.'

'I've got one—two, actually, but one which will go with your blouse,' exclaimed Karen, sliding the doors over Ashley's half of the unit and exhibiting her own. 'Let me see—where is it? Oh, yes, here we are—do you like it?'

The skirt was made of black velvet, long and straight, with only a buckled silver belt to give it any adornment. It was exactly the sort of skirt Ashley needed, and she looked at her cousin rather doubtfully.

'But, Karen, this looks new. Have you worn it yourself?'

Karen made a face. 'Actually, no. It's not really my style. I like something with a bit more—well, with a bit more to it. This is too plain for me, but Mum bought it and I didn't like to say I wasn't keen. I think secretly she's always wanted a daughter who looked like you, but all she got was a facsimile of herself.' She smiled without rancour. 'Wear it! She'll be delighted to think you like it.'

'Oh, I couldn't.' Ashley shook her head. 'Karen, thank you, but no.'

'All right.' Karen shrugged and thrust the skirt back into the wardrobe. 'It's never going to get worn.'

Ashley hesitated. 'Well, if you really mean that——'

'I do.' Karen pulled the skirt out again and handed it to her. 'Go on—wear it! Although why I should encourage you to dress up for Jake Seton, I can't imagine.'

Ashley put down the skirt while she slipped her arms into the sleeves of the green blouse. It was a fine silk blouse that

70

her father had once bought her, and the memory of him caused a frown to mar her brow for a moment. She wondered what he would have thought of Jake Seton, and then banished the notion.

The skirt was a little wide at the waistline, but a pin secured it satisfactorily, and the broad buckled belt hid the small alteration. It was the perfect foil for Ashley's golden colouring and she knew she had never looked more attractive. After examining her reflection she turned for Karen to see and the other girl let out a low wolf whistle.

'Yes, indeed,' she commented admiringly. 'Let Barbara try and improve on that!'

'For the last time, Karen, I'm going out with Mark—and that's all. Just because the others are to be there——' She broke off as she realised Karen was simply not listening to her, and shaking her head turned back to her reflection, fingering the strand of corn-gold hair that fell over one shoulder. 'You don't think I should do something with my hair, do you? Put it up, or plait it?'

'Heavens, no!' Karen was adamant. 'You look super. You have such pretty hair. Don't hide it.'

Ashley shrugged. 'Oh, well, I'm ready. Shall we go down?'

Karen nodded. 'I suppose so. It's ironic, isn't it, that the one night you're going out, I'm not.'

'Why not?'

'Oh, Frank and I had a row—I don't expect I'll be seeing him again.'

'I'm sorry.' Ashley gave her a sympathetic look.

'I'm not,' said Karen, with characteristic ebullience. 'As a matter of fact there's someone else I rather fancy.'

'Who?' Ashley smiled.

'You wouldn't know him. He owns the electric shop in the High Street. His name's Jeffrey Saunders. He came into the Post Office twice yesterday and again this morning, and he talked to me for ages—until old Mrs. Verity shifted him.' She sighed. 'I think he would have asked me for a date if Mrs. Verity hadn't interrupted us. He's rather shy, you see, and I'm sure he was leading up to it.'

Ashley chuckled. 'Well, better luck on Monday.'

'I hope so.' Karen turned out the light and the two girls went downstairs.

Ashley's aunt and uncle both admired her outfit. 'I was beginning to think that skirt was never going to get worn,' exclaimed Mona, as she recognised it, and Karen sent Ashley a look which said *I told you so.*

Mark didn't make any comment when the others were there, although his expression was admiring, but when she went out into the hall to get her suede coat with the fur trimming he followed her, and said: 'You look lovely, Ashley,' in slightly bemused tones.

'Why, thank you, Mark,' she smiled. 'So do you.'

He was looking rather handsome this evening in a blue lounge suit, his fair hair brushed smoothly, and the scent of shaving lo n and hair cream about him.

They were standing smiling at one another, when the side door which opened on to the yard outside shifted slightly and Jake put his head round. When he saw them, his eyes widened and Ashley thought she saw something flicker in their depths for a moment when he contemplated the intimacy of their situation. Then he pushed the door wider and allowed his whole body inside, saying: 'Ah, I see you're ready.'

Mark nodded. 'Yes. Where's Barbara?'

'She's waiting in the car. She didn't want to intrude.' Jake was casual, too casual, Ashley thought, guessing that Barbara had refused to enter the small hotel. 'Shall we go?'

Mona and Karen came to see them off, but David was busy in the bar and could only call a farewell. Outside in the street, a low cream Jaguar nosed the kerb, with Barbara St. John Forrest ensconced comfortably in the front. She smiled faintly at the Suttons and gave them a wave, but she didn't trouble to wind down her window and speak to them.

Mark helped Ashley into the back of the limousine and then slid in beside her, smiling at her in the darkness. Ashley smiled back, but her whole being throbbed with awareness of Jake in the seat in front of her, lean and broodingly attractive in a dark red shirt and charcoal lounge suit.

Barbara was forced to say hello, but her greeting was brief and thereafter it was left to Jake to include his other guests in their conversation. Ashley was glad that Mark seemed to notice nothing amiss, and he and Jake kept a discussion about the day's events at Hislop going until they reached their destination, a large hotel a few miles outside of Bewford.

It was the kind of place that neither Ashley nor Mark would have chosen to visit in the normal way, but obviously Barbara liked it and was well known there. The amount of deference shown to both Jake and his fiancée made Ashley feel rather embarrassed and she was glad when, after shedding their wraps, they entered an attractive cocktail bar.

Immediately, Barbara was hailed by a group of people standing near an artificial cowl-fire in the centre of the floor, and she took Jake's arm, and said: 'It's Barry and Chris! Come along, darling. It's ages since we've seen them.'

'Later, Barbara,' said Jake quietly, but Barbara's lips pursed with annoyance.

'Jake, please,' she insisted. 'They're our friends. We can't ignore them!'

'I have no intention of ignoring them,' returned Jake smoothly. Then to Ashley and Mark: 'What would you like to drink?'

Ashley's fingers were tightly clasped round her evening purse. It was going to be even worse than she had expected, she thought miserably. Barbara hadn't wanted them along, and she was going to make them see it for themselves—if they hadn't done so already.

Mark gave the bar an awkward examination. 'I don't know. What are you having, Ashley?'

Ashley shrugged. 'Tomato juice, please.'

Jake gave her a piercing stare. 'Tomato juice?' he queried dryly.

'That's right.' Ashley refused to look at him, and with an irritated tightening of his lips, he turned to Barbara.

'Your usual, Barbara?'

Barbara's lips were thin. 'I suppose so,' she agreed shortly.

Jake snapped his fingers and a white-coated waiter appeared at his elbow. He ordered their drinks, including a

Bacardi and coke for Mark, and then seemed to force himself to relax as he said:

'Shall we sit down?'

Sitting down necessitated passing the group in the centre of the floor and Ashley and Mark had to stand politely aside while they all greeted Barbara and Jake.

They were all alike, thought Ashley rather wistfully. Rich young socialites who had been born to their unqualified position, totally unaware of any existence except their own. So many things set them apart—the way they dressed, the way they all knew one another, the way they spoke. And Barbara, in her clinging gown of ice-blue crêpe jersey, was very much one of them, standing in their midst, chattering vivaciously about their coming wedding.

But Jake was soon bored. Ashley could see that, at least. He stood to one side of the group, his hands thrust into his pockets, answering in monosyllables when one and another of them tried to draw him into the conversation. Ashley felt an intense sympathy for him, which was stupid in the circumstances, but a sudden weakness invaded her knees when he turned unexpectedly and looked directly at her. He had never looked at her in quite that way before, and suddenly she sensed that what Karen had suggested was not so ridiculous after all. She took a deep breath and looked away, and taking Mark by surprise, said:

'Let's go and sit down, shall we? Er—Jake—Jake and Barbara can join us later. When they've finished talking to their friends.'

'All right.' Mark was willing, and signalling to Jake what they intended to do followed Ashley to a table set in the corner of the room, with wide leather banquettes on either side. 'You're right,' he agreed, sliding on to the seat beside her. 'This is more comfortable.'

Ashley smiled, trying not to look back to where Jake was still standing, but out of the corner of her eye she could see that he was speaking to Barbara and presently they both left the others and came to join Mark and Ashley.

It was fortunate that the two men had the affairs of the estate to discuss, because Barbara was obviously annoyed at being interrupted and said practically nothing. She kept looking back over her shoulder and waving at her friends. Ashley sipped her way through two tomato juices, refused a third and was relieved when Jake suggested that they go into the restaurant for their meal.

To her surprise, there was a group playing in the huge dining room, and a cleared space at the far end indicated that there was entertainment later. Jake's table was close to the cabaret floor and Mark rubbed his hands together enthusiastically.

'I say, this is nice,' he exclaimed, looking round at the busy tables. 'I didn't even know this place existed.'

Jake took the list from the wine waiter and studied its contents thoughtfully. 'It hasn't been open very long,' he commented absently. 'We'll have some champagne—you know what I like.' This to the attentive wine waiter.

'Yes, sir.' The waiter bowed respectfully and went away.

Jake lay back in his seat. 'Now, what do you all want to eat?'

The menus were long and written in French, and Ashley was glad she had a knowledge of that subject. There were so many different courses to choose from, many of them delicacies she had hitherto only read about, that she found it difficult to choose. Mark seemed to find the translation troubling, and kept leaning towards Ashley, asking her what various items were.

Barbara engaged the waiter in conversation concerning her particular likes and dislikes and finally chose the duckling with orange sauce. It was her way of showing, Ashley thought, that she at least was in no way intimidated by her surroundings.

Ashley eventually decided to have lobster and with evident relief Mark said he would have the same. Jake's expression as he watched Mark's easy familiarity with his cousin was strangely enigmatic, and with a brief shrug of his shoulders he asked for a steak for himself.

During the meal, the awkward gaps in the conversation, provoked by Barbara speaking in undertones to her fiancé, were covered by the relaxed music ensuing from the group of musicians on the dais, and as people finished eating they drifted out on to the floor to dance.

75

Ashley found it all rather stimulating. She had never been anywhere like this before. Not even the country club where Jake had taken her on their way back from Raybury, had had facilities for dancing. She had never tasted champagne before either, and although she was only permitted one glass, it all added to the illusion of well-being. She cupped her chin on her hands and watched the dancers, totally unaware of the wistfulness of her expression.

Barbara noticed, though, and gave the younger girl an impatient stare. 'I suppose all this is quite new to you,' she remarked scathingly. 'Personally I can think of places I'd rather be. Bewford is not a particularly exciting place. Give me London for entertainment every time.'

Ashley turned to look at her. 'I used to live in London,' she said. 'It never struck me as being exceptionally exciting. It's just big—and impersonal.'

Barbara's grimace was pitying. 'You're a little young to judge, my dear,' she retorted, in a bored tone.

'It rather depends what one finds exciting, doesn't it?' suggested Jake mildly, offering Mark one of his cheroots.

Barbara rounded on him then. 'You can't find Bewford such an exciting place,' she declared, 'or you wouldn't spend so much time away from it!'

Jake lay back in his chair. 'Places are made up of people!' he remarked distinctly, and Ashley saw Barbara's cheeks flame.

Mark seemed to sense that the conversation was verging on an argument, and putting down the unlit cheroot he got to his feet and said: 'Come along, Ashley. I'm not much of a dancer, but judging by the way everyone's moving, there isn't any room for artistry here.'

Ashley looked up at him in surprise. 'Can we dance?'

'Why not?' Mark made their excuses, and drew her after him on to the floor. But when she was in his arms, he added softly: 'To tell you the truth, I thought those two were about to come to blows and I didn't want to be caught in the crossfire.'

Ashley concentrated on the pale ovals of her nails against his jacket sleeve. 'I don't think Miss St. John Forrest liked having to abandon her friends,' she offered cautiously.

'Perhaps not.' Mark stood on her toe, and apologised at once with a rueful smile. 'But Jake can handle her. He's the only one who can.'

'Yes.'

Ashley tried to sound indifferent, but it came out differently, so that Mark drew back to look down at her in concern. 'You're not letting it upset you, are you, Ash?' he exclaimed, and she shook her head. 'Heavens, it's nothing,' he went on. 'They're always arguing. It's not meant to be taken seriously. They think the world of one another really.'

This news should have cheered her, but it didn't. It merely served to depress her. Her earlier excitement seemed to have dissipated entirely, evaporating like the bubbles in her glass of champagne.

When they got back to the table, however, it was to find that Mark was apparently correct so far as the others were concerned. Barbara was now confiding something into Jake's ear, and from the way she was leaning close to him their contretemps might never have happened, just as Mark had said.

A few minutes later the early floor show was announced and Ashley sat in silence while a male pop singer and a well-known television comedian displayed their individual talents. They went down well with the audience, and even Barbara laughed delightedly at some of the malicious gossip which passed for humour. When it was over, dancing began again and Ashley looked round dejectedly, heaving a deep sigh. She wished someone would suggest leaving. She felt as if she had had enough for one evening.

She looked across the table at Jake and surprised his eyes upon her, a rather grim determination in their depths. She looked away quickly, but was startled into awareness again when his hand descended firmly on her wrist. 'Dance with me!' he demanded, in a curiously strained tone.

Barbara was obviously taken aback by her fiancés' unexpected behaviour, but she said nothing when Jake released Ashley's wrist and rose to his feet. Ashley was trembling. She looked to Mark for guidance, but he was clearly as shocked as Barbara and could merely shake his head in a confused way.

77

Jake was at her side now, looking down at her with those brooding grey eyes of his, forcing her to obey his commands. She was sure that everyone in the room must be staring at them, and when he took her arm in a rather cruel grip and drew her persistently to her feet, there was nothing she could do but go with him.

The minute dance floor was crowded. Jake turned and pulled her into his arms, her hands against the soft mohair of his suit, but now Ashley had to be sensible. 'What on earth made you do a thing like that?' she asked forcefully. 'Your—your fiancée is furious!'

Jake said nothing for a few moments, drawing her into the anonymity of the centre of the floor, his hands sliding intimately down her back to rest on her hips. He was holding her deliberately against him, making her overwhelmingly aware of his disturbing masculinity.

Then he bent his head and rested his forehead against hers, and said quietly: 'Because I had to. Because if I hadn't got you to myself soon, I think I'd have gone quietly out of my mind. Does that answer your question?'

CHAPTER SIX

ASHLEY could not look at him. Her eyes seemed glued to the dark red gleam of his shirt beneath the darker material of his jacket. She was half sure he had not said what she thought he had said, but that didn't stop her from trembling.

'What's wrong?' he asked, lifting his head. 'Are you cold?'

Cold? Ashley could have laughed had it not all been so desperately unfunny.

'No,' she managed. 'I'm not cold.'

How could she be cold with the heat of his hard body burning against hers—with the strength of his arms about her—with the awareness of his desire a tangible thing between them!

'I've frightened you,' he said flatly. 'I'm sorry.'

Ashley looked at him then and caught her breath. No matter how wrong this might be she could not allow him to go on thinking that.

'No,' she said, spreading her fingers against his shoulder. 'I'm not frightened. Why—why should I be?'

He looked down at her. 'You know why,' he replied, and her cheeks flamed. 'We can't talk here, and I want to—talk —to you.'

Common sense reasserted itself. 'I don't think that's a very good idea. I—I'm flattered, of course——'

'*Flattered!*' His voice was grim—angry almost. 'Don't be a silly little girl!'

'But that's what I am, aren't I?' she whispered fiercely, pressing her hands against his chest, putting some space between them. 'Or you wouldn't dare to say such things to me!' And without another word she turned and pushed her way through the throng to the edge of the floor. By the time she reached their table, she was conscious of him behind her, but he made no move to stop her and she sank down into her seat next to Mark with a choking feeling of suffocation.

However, Jake did not sit down. Addressing himself to no one in particular, he said, in what to Ashley's ears sounded bored tones: 'I think it's time we were leaving.' He looked down at Barbara. 'Yes?'

'Oh, indeed,' she answered with feeling, getting to her feet and casting a malicious glance at the younger girl. Then she turned to her fiancé. 'Didn't you enjoy your dance, darling? I thought you would. Ashley was so thrilled that you asked her, just like I said she would be ...'

To Ashley's relief, only her uncle was waiting up for them and apart from asking whether they had enjoyed themselves did not probe too deeply into the events of the evening. Mark had apparently accepted that the dance she had had with Jake had been what Barbara had said—a duty dance, nothing more, and what more reasonable explanation could there be, after all?

But when Ashley was lying stiffly between the sheets, breathing shallowly so as not to disturb Karen, things did not seem so reasonable. There was a sick feeling of apprehension playing havoc with her emotions, and when she finally lost consciousness some few hours later her pillow was damp with the frustrated tears she had shed ...

During the next few days, she tried to behave normally. It was fortunate that Karen was more concerned with promoting her own chances with Jeffrey Saunders than paying any attention to Ashley's subdued appearance, or she might have become suspicious that everything was not as it should be.

On Wednesday, Ashley had her interview at the library. Although she was still feeling rather raw and sensitive, she was able to answer the questions put to her intelligently, and her genuine love of books was sufficient to convince the governors that she was a suitable applicant for the post. Afterwards, Mr. Holt, the chief librarian, shook hands with her and said that he was looking forward to her joining his staff the week after Easter.

She emerged from the building feeling slightly warmer

than when she had gone in, but came to an abrupt standstill when she saw the sleek green sports saloon parked by the kerb, its engine running.

Taking a deep breath, she turned to walk quickly along the pavement, but the car cruised along beside her and the door was thrust open from inside.

'Ashley!' Jake's voice was appealing. 'Please—I want to talk to you.'

Ashley looked desperately round for someone to notice them, but at this hour of the afternoon, on a day when most of the shops in Bewford closed at lunchtime, there were few people about.

'Ashley!' The car stopped and Jake thrust open his door and climbed out, looking at her across the bonnet. 'How did the interview go? Did you get the job?'

Ashley thrust her hands deep into the pockets of her suede coat. 'If you're really interested—yes.'

'I'm glad.' He sounded sincere.

'Why?'

'Because it means you'll be staying in Bewford.'

Ashley looked away from him. 'I may not like the job,' she said, scuffing the toe of her boot.

Jake came round the vehicle. 'Get into the car,' he said quietly. 'Don't make me beg!'

Her cheeks burned. 'And would you?'

'Beg? Yes, if necessary.'

'Oh, Jake—go away!'

She began walking again, but this time he caught her arm. 'Ashley, I want to talk to you.' His voice was thickening now. 'What's so wrong with that? We've talked before.'

Ashley tried to draw away from him, but he was not letting her go. 'We're attracting attention,' she protested in a low tone. 'Please let me go.'

'I don't give a damn,' he snapped. 'Ashley, I *need* to talk to you. Come for a drive with me.'

'I've been warned about going for drives with strange men,' she retorted.

'I am not a strange man. Goddammit, I took you to Raybury, didn't I?'

'That was different. That—was—before——'

'Before I made a fool of myself? All right, say it! I don't mind.' His eyes were hard and cold.

Ashley hesitated. 'Why do you want to talk to me?'

'Get in the car and I'll tell you.'

She sighed. 'Couldn't we just—walk?'

'No.'

Her resistance was ebbing and he sensed it. With a determined hand he opened the nearside door and urged her inside, closing it firmly behind her. Then he walked round and slid in beside her, starting the engine and driving away without speaking.

It was a cold but bright April day. The afternoons were lengthening, and although it was nearing four o'clock it was still sunny. Jake took the moor road, crossing the bridge over the river at the edge of town, and driving up the steep bank to where a cattle grid gave access to the open spaces beyond. She wondered where he was taking her when they drove on, following the winding, uneven track where sheep and goats were a constant hazard. Stretches of gorse and stunted bushes bore witness to the ferocity of the wind in these exposed places where it was possible to drive for miles and find no evident signs of human habitation.

Eventually, up ahead, she saw an enormous outcrop of rock and Jake brought the Ferrari to a smooth halt in the shadow of its bulk. At close quarters, Ashley could see that in fact it was an enormous boulder, but how or why it should be there she had no idea.

And then she became aware that Jake had half turned in his seat to look at her, and all other thoughts were driven from her mind.

'Well?' he challenged quietly. 'Have you nothing to say for yourself?'

Ashley was indignant. 'I understood it was you who wanted to talk,' she retorted.

'Oh, yes.'

He looked down as he unfastened the buttons of the jacket of the cream denim suit he was wearing. Ashley's eyes were drawn to his hands, long-fingered brown hands, which she knew could exert pain without much effort. Beneath his jacket he was wearing a cream silk shirt, and she thought how well his clothes fitted him. The fine material of the shirt clung to his skin in places and she guessed he wore nothing beneath it. To her horror, she found herself wondering whether he had hair on his chest, and looked away in alarm. She had never been interested in the physical appearance of any man before, and there was something vaguely wanton about even pondering such thoughts.

He moved then and she felt his thigh against hers, the warmth of his silk-clad body against her back. Her breathing was becoming constricted and the suffocated feeling she had felt that night in the hotel had returned in full force. Why was he doing this? she asked herself desperately. Didn't he realise that she was aware of him with every fibre of her being?

'Aren't you warm in that thick coat?' he asked, against her ear, and she almost jumped out of her skin.

'What? Oh—oh, no—not very,' she stammered, angry with herself for reacting so violently to him.

'I think you are,' he insisted. 'Take it off.'

Her answer was to draw the collar of her coat closer about her ears and with a shrug he moved away from her to rest against the door at his side of the vehicle.

Ashley ventured a look at him, aware that she half regretted his removal of himself. He was sitting staring moodily down at the ring on the smallest finger of his right hand, and there was a disturbing air of melancholy about him. Unwillingly, she wanted to do what he had asked, and with unsteady fingers she unfastened her coat and wriggled out of it, flinging it into the back.

He looked at her then, and the look in his eyes was dark and disruptive. Her purple woollen skirt had ridden up over her thighs and she smoothed it down nervously, making unnecessary adjustments to the ribbed edge of her purple sweater. She was filled with a desire to move closer to him, to touch him, and the knowledge was terrifying.

The raucous cry of a gull wheeling effortlessly over the gorse distracted her, and she took a deep calming breath. What was the matter with her? Was this what the girls at school whispered about? Was she no better than they were —worse perhaps, because apart from other things, Jake was engaged to be married to somebody else, had been all along.

'Wh-what is this stone?' she jerked out, looking up at the immense boulder beside them, trying to ignore the tension between them.

Jake moved lithely away from the door, one arm along the back of her seat. 'It's called the Witchstone,' he replied. 'It's one of the last remaining remnants of the Ice Age. But people are superstitious in these parts, and it's been endowed with supernatural powers down the years. No one can say with any surety how it got its name.'

'I see.' She fidgeted with the neckline of her sweater. 'It's fascinating, isn't it? I—I've read about such things, of course. I remember once seeing a stone like it—but smaller —and it was supposed to be a meteorite—a falling star——'

His fingers closed round the nape of her neck under the weight of her hair. 'Be quiet!' he commanded harshly. 'I didn't bring you up here to talk about—falling stars—ancient relics! I wanted you to know that what I said the other evening, I meant!'

Ashley's lips parted incredulously. She bent her head so that the veil of her hair hid her expression. 'Mr. Seton, I think this has gone too far——'

Hard fingers looped her hair back behind one ear, and his hand forced her face up to his. 'You're wrong!' he stated emphatically. 'It hasn't gone far enough.'

Ashley moved uneasily in his grasp. 'I think you should take me back now, Mr. Seton.'

'My name is Jake, and you know it!'

She spread a helpless hand. 'Please—look, I don't know how you regard the girls in—in Bewford. I know your family wouldn't approve of your associating—I mean—well, whatever your personal feelings are, I—I'm not interested.' She licked her dry lips. 'I—I can't speak for anyone else, of course——'

His eyes glittered dangerously. 'Just what the hell are you trying to say?'

She shook her head. 'You know what I'm trying to say,' she exclaimed. 'I—I—maybe in the past the girls you've—you've known—have jumped at the chance of going out with you—of being able to boast to their friends—*oh*!'

84

She broke off on a cry of protest as his fingers on her nape tightened painfully. She had never seen anyone look so angry before, and a twinge of fear at the realisation of their isolation pricked her.

'You think this is common practice for me, is that it?' he demanded savagely. 'You think that I exercise the old rights of the squire to know the choicest maiden before anyone else, am I right?'

Ashley was terribly embarrassed. 'I—I didn't say that——'

'That was what you meant, wasn't it? "Know" being the operative word, I suppose. And are you aware what *know* means, innocent as you are? It means——'

'I know what it means!' Ashley pressed her palms over her ears. 'Stop it! Stop saying things like this!'

'Why? Isn't it what you expect me to say?'

'No—yes—oh, I don't know.' Her lips trembled. 'Please —take me home! I—I don't know what—what you want of me, but—but whatever it is—it's no use!' She brushed a hand across her eyes. 'I'm afraid I'm not—experienced where men are concerned.'

'I am aware of that.' His eyes narrowed. 'I'm not completely without sensibilities, you know.'

Ashley drew a shaking breath. 'Then why did you bring me here?'

'Well, not for the sordid little reasons buzzing round in your head,' he snapped coldly, withdrawing his arm from behind her and settling lower in his seat. 'Old-fashioned as it may seem to you, I do not make a habit of seducing schoolgirls in cars. In fact, strangely enough, I don't seduce schoolgirls at all. But when the need for sex is on me, I prefer the comfort of a bed——'

'Oh, please!'

'What's wrong? Have I shocked you? I don't see why. You have one hell of an opinion of me. I'd like to know what I've done to deserve such a reputation!'

Ashley bent her head. 'Well, there—there's Barbara. You can't deny that.'

'I don't.'

She looked up. 'And doesn't she deserve your loyalty?'

'Maybe.'

'Well then——'

'Well what?' He glared at her dispassionately. 'Am I not a human being? Am I not allowed failings? One failing, at least.'

'What do you mean?'

'What do you think I mean, you frightened child?' He half turned towards her, his eyes cold and angry. 'Do you want me to tell you? Do you want me to bare my soul before you? Would that give you a thrill? Is that the sort of vicarious experience you want?'

Ashley shook her head. 'I don't understand you. You're deliberately confusing me.'

'I'm deliberately destroying myself before you!' He bit out the words, as though despising himself for speaking them.

Ashley didn't know what to say—what to do. He had the power to make her feel the aggressor—to fill her with a sense of compassion towards him. And something else— something she dared not acknowledge even to herself.

'Jake,' she began awkwardly, 'I'm sorry if I've offended you——'

'Offended me?' He gave her a contemptuous stare. 'Why should you think you've done that?'

Ashley made a helpless gesture. 'Stop trying to put me in the wrong. You are engaged to Barbara. You can't deny that. So why are you—well, being like this with me?'

'How would you like me to be?' His eyes were shaded by his long lashes.

'Well, like that day we went to Raybury. We—we could talk then.'

'And we can't now?'

'No.'

'And why do you suppose that is?'

'Because—because you've—you've changed things.'

'*I've* changed things?'

'Well, I haven't.'

'Haven't you?' There was a sensual curve to his mouth. 'You mean that were I to withdraw what I said the other evening, you could go on being—the same?'

86

'I—I don't know. I should remember what had been said.'

'But what of it? If it meant nothing to you, why think about it?'

She turned away from him. His reasoning was illogical. How could she forget what he had said? How could she ignore the implications behind their relationship? And *oh, God!* she didn't want to ignore them!

She felt him move suddenly and a draught of cold air entered the car. She swung round and found that he had got out, standing looking across the wild expanses of shrub and gorse, hands thrust into the pockets of his denim jacket.

She swallowed hard. It was over. All she had to do now was wait for him to get back in and he would drive back to Bewford and that would be the last she would see of him. She knew it as clearly as if it had been put into words. And the knowledge sickened her ...

How could she let it end like this? Inexperienced as she was, surely this longing for him that she had was more than mere physical attraction. If she confided her feelings to anyone they would think she was mad. After all, Jake was twelve years older than she was, experienced and mature; using her as a final experience before the bands of marriage bound themselves about him.

The feeling of suffocation that came with these thoughts sent waves of heat through her body. She felt as though she was choking in the warm atmosphere of the car. She had to get out. She had to free herself of this awful stifling feeling.

She thrust open her door and got out, scarcely aware of Jake turning to look at her, a frown marring his lean attractive face. She stumbled away from the car in the opposite direction from where he was standing, leaving the road to step through the undergrowth, uncaring that her boots were getting scratched in the process. She took great gulping breaths of air, shivering a little as a chilling sense of despair enveloped her.

A blue line on the horizon heralded the deepening shadows of late afternoon, and a cool little breeze whistled with eerie mournfulness round the Witchstone. It would be evening soon. Aunt Mona would be preparing their meal, eagerly awaiting news of Ashley's interview. If only she had gone straight home—if only she had not come up here—not agreed to Jake's invitation. The fact that she had not agreed in so many words was immaterial. He had known she had been unsure of herself—had half wanted to come with him.

Scufflings in the heather a few yards away revealed themselves as a pair of grouse, no doubt disturbed by Ashley's progress. The moors were alive with creatures of all kinds —pheasants and wild fowl, hares, rabbits, foxes; it was a wildlife sanctuary, disturbed only in the season by shooting parties.

She wrapped her arms across herself, knowing that she would have to go back to the car soon. And yet she put off the moment of so doing. It was incredible to think that a little over three months ago she had scarcely heard of Bewford—let alone Jake Seton.

She was so absorbed with her thoughts, so remote from the world around her that when another bird came fluttering up out of the heather just ahead of her she was really startled. She gave a cry and stepped awkwardly backwards, losing her balance as her heel went down a rabbit hole. She felt an agonising pain as her ankle twisted and collapsed to her knees with a gasp. The winter-hard twigs of gorse and thorn hurt her legs, laddering her tights and digging mercilessly into her palms as she tried to save herself. It was the last straw, but she fought back the tears that came to her eyes and was on her feet again before Jake could reach her. He came striding slowly across the space between them with obvious reluctance, his suede boots crunching the brittle shoots underfoot. He halted just before her, his eyes showing only faint traces of concern.

'Are you all right?' he asked curtly, and she nodded her head.

'Yes. I—I must have tripped in a rabbit hole or something.' She tentatively tried her weight on her injured foot and drew back sharply as a shaft of fire seemed to envelop her leg. 'I twisted my ankle.'

Jake considered her appearance critically. 'You look a mess!' he announced, with some derision, and she caught her breath indignantly.

'So would you if you'd just fallen down a rabbit hole,' she declared with feeling. 'Oh—oh, how gallant! *You look a mess!* Not—is your ankle painful—or can you make it to the car! Nothing helpful or constructive, but just setting me down in the most cruel way!' Her voice broke on a sob, and rather than let him see her cry, she turned away and began to limp painfully towards the Ferrari.

Jake followed her, his hands thrust deep into the pockets of his jacket, his expression brooding. Ashley was feeling quite sick by the time she reached the car, and she leant weakly against the bonnet, wishing she had had the sense to remain inside instead of venturing across the moor. How different life was from what the novelists would like it to be, she thought miserably. In the best traditions of romance, Jake should have swept her up into his arms and carried her to the car, comforting her tenderly, showing her how much he needed her. Instead, he had displayed a distinct lack of concern—had even spoken contemptuously to her.

Now he swung open her door with controlled politeness and indicated that she should get inside. She would have liked to have been able to refuse. To pull her coat out of the back and tell him she would make her own way home. But even had her ankle not been throbbing with a sickening intensity, she could not have done it. They were miles from Bewford, and the moor at night was no place for anyone alone.

She straightened, wincing as she did so, and for the first time he noticed her pallor and the beads of perspiration on her forehead. His eyes dropped down the length of her body to rest thoughtfully on her ankle, and then he said: 'It really is painful?' in questioning tones.

Ashley clenched her fists. 'No. *No!* Whatever gave you that idea?'

He ignored her, and going down on his haunches put his hands round her injured ankle. Whether the throbbing heat of the injury penetrated even the leather of her boot she could not be certain, but his expression changed and he rose abruptly to his feet.

'I'm sorry,' he said, somewhat stiffly. 'I thought you were playing for sympathy.'

Her eyes sought his angrily. 'Am I supposed to accept that as an apology?'

'That's entirely up to you.'

She stared at him helplessly, frustratedly aware that she was not reaching him. He was the same man, and yet he might have been a stranger for all the effect her remarks had on him.

'Oh, Jake!' she cried despairingly, and as though that agonised little appeal broke through the cold façade he had erected between them, she saw the darkening of emotion in his eyes.

'Get in the car, Ashley!' he commanded, standing aside to allow her to do so, but she could not let it go.

'Jake, please! Don't be like this. I—I can't stand it——'

His fists clenched for a moment. 'You can't stand it?' he snapped. 'I, of course, can.'

Her lips parted. 'Jake, what is it you want of me?'

He stepped closer to her. 'Don't tempt me to show you, rabbit!' he muttered. 'Perhaps it was rough justice—your twisting your ankle in a *rabbit* hole!'

Ashley gasped. 'How can you be so—so cruel?' she exclaimed, and gripping tightly at the bonnet she turned away from him.

He moved so that he was directly behind her. The warmth of his body enveloped her, warming her. She could smell the faint aroma of his after-shaving lotion, and something else—the faint, musky scent of his body, and she succumbed to the desire which had been plaguing her all afternoon, she leant back—against him.

For a moment he was completely still and all she could feel was the strong beat of his heart against her shoulder. But then his hands gripped her waist, sliding possessively round and across her stomach, pressing her back against him with increasing urgency. She felt him tremble as his mouth touched the smooth curve of her neck, and his voice was thickening with emotion as he said: 'Ashley, Ashley—I'm sorry.'

'Don't be,' she breathed unsteadily. 'But please—kiss me. Really kiss me . . .'

He turned her to face him, looking down at her with

troubled eyes, but it was she who was trembling when his mouth finally found hers. 'Relax,' he urged, against her lips. 'Open your mouth—don't fight me——'

Ashley had never been kissed in passion before. The few kisses she had received from the moist lips of boys at school had repelled her, and her instincts were to keep her lips and teeth clamped tightly together. But his lips coaxed them apart and she forgot all about her ankle, forgot everything and everybody in a deepening surge of pure physical enjoyment. She was close against Jake's body, she could feel his muscles straining against hers, her breasts were crushed against his chest, and his thighs were hard against her legs. His mouth wasn't soft, but firm and compellingly male, and an awful wanton weakness possessed her, silencing her conscience. There was something wholly satisfying about putting her arms under his jacket, next to his silk-clad skin, and knowing that she was capable of arousing him like this.

But at last, with reluctance, Jake propelled her some distance away from him, raking his hands through his hair. Now there was a definite line of strain around his mouth, and he adjusted his tie with hands that were not quite steady. Then he looked at Ashley, and where she had been half afraid she would find contempt she found a disturbing tenderness, an aching sweetness that did peculiar things to her nervous system.

'I think we must get back,' he spoke quietly, obviously trying to behave normally. 'I can't take you home looking as you do. We'll go to a friend of mine's and you can tidy yourself before I deliver you to your aunt, yes?'

Ashley frowned, but Jake was urging her into the car and she got inside obediently, watching him as he walked round to slide in beside her. Her ankle was not quite so painful as it had been before, and now that common sense was re-asserting itself she had other more sophisticated tortures to suffer. The situation had not changed. Just because he had kissed her, just because he had shown her that he was not quite in control of himself where she was concerned, it did not alter the fact of his engagement, the fact that any association he might have with her could only be of a temporary nature. Was she prepared to accept that? Was she prepared to accept that because she felt something for him, something which hitherto had been unknown to her, she must always live on the fringes of his life, constantly in the shadows—the other woman, in fact?

She felt her nails biting into the palms of her hands. It was ludicrous. She was all kinds of a fool. She was allowing her physical attraction towards him to blind her to his faults, the way he could so blithely make love to her without any apparent thought for his fiancée. Had he no conscience? Didn't he care that they might be observed together? That someone might conceivably put two and two together and come up with the right answer?

Jake was adjusting his clothes to make himself more comfortable before starting the car, and she turned to him reluctantly, biting her lips to stop them from trembling.

'Jake——'

'Yes?' He looked at her, his eyes warm and caressing.

'I—I—perhaps you'd better just take me home——'

'Why?'

She bit her lips harder so that a little spurt of blood showed momentarily against her white teeth. 'We—we might be seen together. It—it would be awkward——'

'For whom?' There was coolness in his voice now.

'Oh, for you, of course,' she cried impatiently. 'What could it matter to me?'

Jake's expression softened and his arm slid behind her, drawing her resistingly towards him. 'Don't make me show you what a fool you are,' he murmured against her hair. 'Right now I might not behave as a gentleman should.' He smoothed her flushed cheeks with a probing finger. 'Don't you realise I don't give a damn who sees us together? I want people to see us together. I want them to talk about us. Perhaps then when the news is out, it won't come as so much of a surprise to them.'

'News? What news?' She stared up at him in surprise.

'The news of my broken engagement, of course,' he told her briefly, pushing her gently but firmly away from him. Then he leant forward and started the engine, turning the car expertly and driving back towards Bewford while Ashley sat in a stunned silence ...

CHAPTER SEVEN

BEFORE they reached the outskirts of Bewford, Jake turned off the main road on to a side turning which ran for some distance between tall hedges before coming to a gate marked *Private*. Leaving the engine running, he got out and opened the gate, and then after driving through closed it behind him. Ashley wondered where he was taking her, who was this person he regarded as a friend. But after the statement he had made before leaving the Witchstone, she felt unable to voice her anxieties. Instead, she sat stiffly in her seat, sure this must all be some particularly cruel game he was playing.

Although she didn't yet know the countryside around Bewford too well, she had the feeling that they were now in the Seton estate. She thought parts of it looked familiar. After all, she had been there with Mark, and her nerves tightened in alarm. Surely he didn't intend taking her to the Hall looking like this!

But to her relief, he turned the car towards a building just visible among a clump of elms, and as they drew nearer she saw it was a white-painted cottage with a golden Labrador lying lazily on the path. However, the dog came bounding towards them as Jake stopped the car, and after a casual look in Ashley's direction, he got out and bent to fondle the animal.

'Hello, Bess, old girl!' he said, laughing as the dog tried to lick his face. 'Where's Joe?'

Ashley hesitated, and then she too got out, wincing a little as her injured foot encountered the ground. She was overwhelmingly conscious of her untidy appearance, and reached back into the car for her coat. She was putting it on when a man emerged from the cottage and came to greet them. He was a tall man, and walked without the aid of a stick, but his mass of grey hair and the lines on his face belied the fact that he must be in his seventies. He grinned welcomingly when he recognised Jake, and hailed him heartily.

'Well, well. So you've finally found the time to come and see me!'

Jake grinned in return. 'It's only been a couple of weeks, Joe,' he protested good-naturedly. 'And I have had plenty to do. You know I come up here as often as I can.'

Joe acknowledged this with a wry nod of his head, and then looked curiously at Ashley. She was bending now, stroking the Labrador, talking to her reassuringly.

'Who's this?' he asked, without preamble. 'The girl you were telling me about?'

Jake looked across at Ashley and nodded. 'Yes, this is Ashley. Ashley, I'd like you to meet Joe Pearson. He's been gamekeeper for my father for as long as I can remember.'

Ashley came forward to shake hands with the old man, conscious of the penetration of his gaze. For all his age, his eyes were blue and piercing, and she had the feeling he was assessing her very thoroughly. But really all that registered in her mind was the fact that he knew of her—that Jake had mentioned her to him. What did it mean?

'So you're the young woman who's been causing my boy sleepless nights, are you?' he asked disconcertingly, and Ashley flushed.

'I—I don't know about that——' she began awkwardly, and he snorted.

'Don't you? Then perhaps you should.' He glanced at Jake, whose expression was rather enigmatic, and then nodded towards the cottage. 'Well, come along in. The kettle's on, and no doubt it's boiling its head off by now.' He glanced down at Ashley's scratched hands and legs. 'What you been doing with her, boy?'

It was strange hearing Jake being called a boy, but he didn't seem to object. He took Ashley by the shoulders and pushed her gently before him into the cottage, saying as he did so: 'I'm not responsible. She did it all herself. But she's twisted her ankle, and maybe some cold water wouldn't come amiss.'

Inside the cottage, Ashley looked about her with interest. The whitewashed walls were hung with horse brasses, and there was an enormous hearth, with a black-leaded fire and an oven adjoining it. There was a kettle singing on the hob over a roaring log fire, and the flames leaping up the chimney cast shadows over the oak settle, and chintz-covered furniture.

'Sit you down,' said Joe, going to the sink and running some water from the one tap it boasted into a bowl. 'Take off her boot, lad, and let's have a look at it.'

Ashley found herself sitting on the chintz-covered settee, while Jake knelt to unfasten her boot. 'No—no, really. I can do it,' she protested, and pushed his hand away, fumbling with the zip herself. Actually, it was much less painful now, but when she drew off the boot she saw that it was swollen.

Jake shrugged and rose to his feet, and she found it difficult not to look at him and go on looking at him. Already her senses were leaping at the devastating knowledge that he was not teasing her—that he really did find her attractive, desirable . . .

She brought herself up short. Joe was kneeling at her feet with a sponge and a bowl of cold water and was saying: 'Can't you take off your stockings, lass? If I'm going to put a compress on that ankle, it needs to be next to the skin.'

'Oh, really, do you think that's necessary?' She managed a smile. 'I—it feels much better than it did.' She glanced round. 'If I could just wash my hands and comb my hair——'

Joe wrinkled his nose at her. 'Now surely you're not going to tell me you're afraid to take off your stockings in front of Jake, are you? You young people—I thought you were completely without modesty.'

'Not Ashley,' remarked Jake dryly. 'But if I'm in the way, I'll wait outside.'

Ashley sighed. 'They're not stockings—they're tights.'

Joe got to his feet. 'Well now, there's a bedroom upstairs. Do you think you could make it?'

Ashley nodded vigorously. 'I'm sure I could. But really——'

'Come along, then.' Joe was opening a door at the back of the kitchen and behind it she saw a flight of crooked stairs leading upward. 'That's the way. You come down when you're ready. You'll find some cold water in a jug on my washstand, and there's a comb too, if you need one.'

'I—I have a comb, thank you.' With a flustered look at Jake, Ashley made her way up the stairs, finding a tiny landing at the top from which opened two doors. Not knowing which was Joe's bedroom, Ashley opened the first only to find a small boxroom, but the second proved to be the one she wanted.

The bedroom was like the living room downstairs. Whitewashed walls, a couple of brasses and a hand-woven tapestry of a famous proverb, cotton rugs on the wooden floor, and an iron double bed with a fringed cotton coverlet; plain and simple, but attractive for all that.

There was a jug and basin on the washstand as Joe had said, and Ashley washed her hands, wincing at the icy water. Then she took off her other boot and stripped off the laddered tights. She would go home without any stockings. At least that way she would not draw attention to her legs.

Thinking about home, she looked at her watch and saw to her horror it was after half past five. Good heavens, Aunt Mona would be wondering where she was. Her interview had been at three o'clock. Whatever would the family be thinking?

Stuffing the torn tights into her bag, she drew out a comb and dragged it painfully through the tangled length of her hair. A shiver of excitement would not be denied when she remembered how Jake had buried his face in her hair, had tangled it round his fingers, holding her mouth to his . . .

She pushed the comb away, angry at the way her hands trembled as she did so. She must stop thinking about him all the time. It was not good for her nervous system, feeling her emotions constantly at fever pitch.

Downstairs, Jake and Joe were talking quietly together, but they both looked round when Ashley re-entered the room.

'Did you manage?' asked Joe, getting up from his seat to make room for her on the settee beside Jake.

'Yes, but as you can see, my ankle's fine.'

'A little cold bandage will just put that right,' insisted

Joe, and Jake reached out and caught her hand, pulling her down beside him.

'Let him do it,' he murmured softly. 'He wants to.' His eyes rested sensuously on her mouth. 'What's the rush? Don't you like it here?'

Ashley took a deep breath. 'Of course I do. But—but Aunt Mona will be worried. I should have been home a couple of hours ago.'

Jake's thumb caressed her palm. 'She'll have to get used to it,' he remarked, with a certain amount of arrogance. 'And pretty soon, you may have a different home.'

Ashley dragged her hand away from him as Joe came back to wind a cold stretch bandage around the injured ankle. After the initial chill of coldness, it was rather soothing, and she realised that once she had left Jake, once this over-stimulated feeling of intoxication he was filling her with left her, she would doubtless be glad of the support.

The tea was already made and brewing in a brown pot on the hearth and even Ashley knew they could not leave without having some. And besides, had it not been for her concern for Aunt Mona, there was something infinitely desirable about sitting there in the firelit room, drinking tea, with Jake's shoulder resting companionably against hers.

But at last Jake said they must go, and they all went to the door together, the Labrador, Bess, leaping about them.

'You must come again, lass,' said Joe, shaking Ashley's hand warmly. 'I don't get many visitors here, and I'd be glad to see someone as young and attractive as you.'

Ashley smiled tremulously, glowing inside. 'Thank you, Mr. Pearson——'

'Joe—please!'

'All right—Joe.' She glanced at Jake. 'I'd like to come again. When—when we don't have to hurry away.'

'There you are then, Jake. It's up to you.' Joe patted the younger man familiarly on the shoulder.

'We'll be back,' promised Jake easily, taking Ashley's hand firmly in his.

'And—and thank you,' added Ashley. 'For the compress.'

'It was nothing, lass,' Joe nodded, grinning. 'Cheerio.'

The Ferrari moved away slowly, and Ashley waved until the trees hid the cottage from view. Then she sank back in her seat and heaved a deep sigh.

'It wasn't so bad, was it?' queried Jake mockingly, and she shook her head, tempted to snuggle against him. She felt warm and comforted, like a cat, and her instincts were to show it.

Putting her hand tentatively on his thigh, she said: 'Jake—can I ask you something?'

'Anything you like,' he replied, putting his hand over hers.

She paused, still unsure of herself, and he said quietly: 'Do you want clarification of what I've said so far?'

'Hmm.' She nodded, drawing her legs up under her and moving closer to him.

Jake's fingers tightened on the wheel. 'All right. Since I met you, I've thought of nothing else—no one else.' He sighed. 'Surely it's been painfully obvious, the puerile excuses I've made to see you.'

'Karen said that,' exclaimed Ashley involuntarily, and Jake shrugged.

'Karen's a very astute girl. And more experienced than you are, I guess.'

'But—but you're engaged to Barbara!'

'Barbara and I are through—finished.'

'You can't be serious!'

'Why not?' His eyes darkened. 'Oh, don't worry, I'm not blaming you entirely for that. Nor does it place you in any position of obligation——'

'Obligation!' She stared at him helplessly. 'Oh, Jake, what's that supposed to mean?'

He stopped the car to open the gate they had entered by and not until it was closed again and they were driving towards the main road did he say: 'I realise that you're very young—that you may not feel as I do. But I don't believe you're indifferent to me either.'

'Indifferent?' Ashley sank back weakly on to her heels. 'Oh, Jake!' She shook her head helplessly.

Jake slowed as he approached the major road. 'You were right in one way. I have—known—one or two women.' He half closed his eyes. 'No—God! I've known a lot of women. It's pretty common in the circles I move in.' He glanced sideways at her. 'Does that shock you?'

She wriggled round in her seat, folding her hands in her lap. 'Shock me? I—I don't know. Should it?'

He sighed. 'Virginity is usually scandalised by promiscuity.' He shrugged. 'I admit, that was what first attracted me to you—your shyness, your outraged modesty. I wanted to make love to you from the very beginning. I still do.'

Her face burned. 'I must seem very ignorant.'

'Ignorant? No.' He half smiled. 'Innocent, yes.' He gave her another devastating look. 'I love you, Ashley. And I've never said that to any woman and meant it.'

Ashley's tongue probed her upper lip. 'But—but how do I know you mean it now?'

Jake's eyes narrowed. 'You don't. You'll have to take it on trust. But I'll tell you one thing—damning though it might seem in your eyes—if I didn't love you, you wouldn't still be the innocent creature you are.'

Her eyes were indignant. 'How can you say that?'

He smiled. 'There's a saying about there being ways...'

They were crossing the bridge over the river and running along the embankment before turning into the High Street. They would be at the Golden Lion in less than a minute and Ashley was not ready for it. She rubbed her moist palms against the sides of her skirt, and ran a hasty hand over her hair.

'You look perfectly satisfactory,' he remarked in a dry voice. 'No one will know unless you choose to tell them.'

Ashley gave him a frustrated look. 'What am I to tell them?'

'That's up to you.'

'Jake—help me!'

'Do you want me to come in with you?'

'No!' She swallowed hard. 'No, not yet. I—I—oh, Jake, when am I going to see you again?'

'When do you want to see me again?'

She closed her eyes for a brief moment. 'I don't want to leave you,' she confessed huskily, and his hand closed over her knee possessively.

'Good. That's how I feel. Good feeling, isn't it?'

'I don't know.' She glanced round desperately. 'Oh, heavens, we're there.' She pressed her fingers tightly over his. 'Did you really mean it? About loving me, I mean?'

'Want me to prove it?' His mouth mocked her.

She held his gaze for a long moment and then allowed her heart to expand. 'I think I should like that,' she breathed, and thrust open her door.

Jake was out of the car and round beside her almost before she had chance to retrieve her coat from the back. He took the garment from her, slinging it round her shoulders and drawing her towards him with the two sides. Then he bent his head and pressed a lingering kiss on her mouth.

She drew back from him almost at once, her eyes darting this way and that in alarm. 'Jake! Anyone could see us!'

'So?' His expression was indulgent. 'You shouldn't say things like that if you don't expect some kind of a reaction. Now, how about dinner this evening?' He consulted his watch. 'In say—half an hour from now.'

Ashley shook her head, and as she did so she saw Karen and Jeffrey Saunders coming towards them, only a few yards distant. Her heart plunged. Had they noticed what had been happening between Jake and herself? Knowing Karen, it would be unusual if they had not.

'Karen's coming,' she whispered fiercely. 'I expect she saw us. What will she think?'

'Do you care?' Jake tipped his head on one side. 'She'll have to know sooner or later, won't she?'

'Well—yes, I suppose so.'

'There you are, then.' Jake released her and she turned to her cousin, feeling absurdly embarrassed.

Karen was looking absolutely astounded, and Ashley didn't need to speculate any longer over whether she had seen them. She obviously had, and she stared at her cousin with undisguised impatience.

But Jake, with his innate confidence, was far from disconcerted. 'Hello, Karen,' he greeted her lazily. 'Saunders. How are you?'

'I—er—I'm fine, thank you, Jake. Er—you know Jeff, don't you?' Karen was curt.

'Sure,' Jake nodded amiably. 'How's business?'

Jeffrey Saunders was a shy young man, but he knew precisely who Jake was and he smiled in a polite way and said that everything was going very satisfactorily. Jake said: 'Good' and for a few moments they all stood looking at one another. Then Karen, realising that Jake was not about to be intimidated, excused herself and Jeffrey and led the way into the hotel, but not before she had cast a rather disapproving look in Ashley's direction which conveyed all too clearly what she thought about the affair.

When the door had swung closed behind them, Ashley shifted her weight from one foot to the other, and said: 'I must go in. Aunt Mona will be positively furious when Karen tells her I'm just outside.'

Jake sighed. 'And dinner?'

'Oh—I don't think I can.'

'Why?' There was a trace of impatience in his voice now.

'You know why. I—I have to go in. I have to tell them what happened this afternoon. Aunt Mona will have a meal ready for me. I can't disappoint her.'

Jake thrust his hands into his trousers pockets. 'And me?'

Ashley looked up at him tremulously. 'You know I'd rather be with you.'

Jake half turned away. 'All right, all right. Tomorrow, then. Lunch?'

'I'll be at school,' she volunteered quietly.

'Is that necessary?'

'I'm afraid it is. I—I have to tell Miss Kincaid what happened, too.'

'I see. You still intend to take that job at the library, then.'

Ashley frowned. 'Of course.'

'I see.'

'What else could I do?' She stared at him, her eyes troubled.

'What indeed?' He walked to the car. 'I'll be seeing you.'

She watched him slide behind the wheel and then panic overcame her inhibitions and she ran to the window, tapping on it urgently. He rolled the window down and looked at her between the long black lashes, his expression hard to discern.

'Jake?' she murmured tentatively.

'Yes.' At any other time his tone would have discouraged her, but not now, not knowing him as she did.

'When—when will I see you?' She spoke quietly.

Jake's lips twisted. 'I don't know. When you're free, I guess.'

'When *I'm* free!'

'Well, it's not easy to pin you down, is it?'

'Oh, Jake!' She shook her head. 'That's not true.'

'I do have some commitments of my own,' he added.

Ashley felt a lump in her throat. 'I'm sorry.' She turned away. 'Goodnight, then.'

'Goodnight.'

The Ferrari roared away and feeling positively drained of emotion, Ashley entered the hotel.

Her aunt was in the kitchen with Karen. 'Well, this is a fine time to be coming home——' she began sharply as Ashley came through the door. Then she saw the girl's white face. 'Why—Ashley? What is it? What's wrong? Are you ill?'

'I—I think I'm going to be sick,' announced Ashley faintly, and reached the sink only just in time.

Karen helped her upstairs afterwards and sat on the bed watching as Ashley removed her coat. Then Ashley sat down and began to remove her boots, flushing as Karen noticed she was not wearing any tights.

'He didn't rape me, if that's what you're thinking,' she declared in a somewhat unsteady voice. 'I—I twisted my ankle and laddered my tights. So—so we went to the home of a friend of his, and he put this bandage on my foot.'

Karen shook her head. 'Is it all right now.'

Ashley nodded. 'Yes. The pain's almost gone. It's just a little swollen, that's all. I can take this off.'

'But what were you doing with Jake in the first place?'

Ashley tugged a brush through her tangled hair. 'He—took me for a drive. To—to the Witchstone. I'd never been there before.'

'Fancy!' Karen was sarcastic.

102

'You think I'm a fool, don't you?'

'I don't know what to think. I couldn't believe my eyes when I saw him kissing you outside. He was kissing you, wasn't he?'

'Did you tell Aunt Mona?'

'The details, you mean? Heavens, no. I just said you were outside talking to Jake. I had to say something. Jeff was with me.'

'Oh, yes.' Ashley turned from the mirror. 'Where is he?'

'Jeff? He's with Dad. They get on very well together, or hadn't you noticed?'

Ashley turned back to her reflection, running her finger-tips across her cheekbones. 'Well—thanks, anyway.'

'Don't thank me. I want nothing to do with it. I'd just like to know what you think you're doing getting involved with him.'

Ashley sighed. 'I think—I'm in love with him!'

'*Glory!*' Karen flopped back on the bed, putting her palms to her cheeks. 'You must be crazy!'

'Why?' Ashley tried to sound unconcerned.

'You know the answer to that as well as I do.' Karen propped herself up on her elbows. 'There's no future in it.'

Ashley bent her head. 'He said—he said he'd broken his engagement to Barbara.'

'What?' Karen sat right up then.

'You heard what I said.' Ashley tried to quell the rising sense of nervous tension that played such havoc with her physical condition.

Karen frowned. 'Well, I haven't heard of it. But maybe that's not so surprising. Wednesday is our quietest day, after all.'

'Do you think it's true?' Ashley's eyes were troubled.

'Don't you?'

'I don't know. He—he said—he loved me.'

Karen gave an exasperated snort. 'Oh, did he? Well, let me tell you, that won't be the first time he's said that to a girl!'

'I know. He told me so himself. But he said he means it this time.'

Karen grimaced. 'And you believe him, I suppose.'

'I don't know what to believe.'

'Are you going to tell Mum?'

Ashley turned away. 'I don't know—I don't know if I can.'

'When are you seeing him again?'

'I don't know that either.'

'Why not?'

'I—I'm afraid he—he left rather—angrily.'

'Why? Because I saw you two together? I've told you, Ashley——'

'*No!*' Ashley spoke fiercely. 'Not for those reasons. Quite the opposite, in fact.'

'Opposite?'

'Yes. He—he would have come in with me—he would have told Aunt Mona himself.'

Karen was clearly impressed now. 'You mean that was why he was kissing you in the street? To show he didn't care who saw?'

'Partly, I suppose.'

'Oh, Ashley!' Karen shook her head slowly. 'Why didn't you let him do it then?'

'Because—because—oh, I don't know. It seemed so premature, somehow. I haven't had time to take it all in myself yet. I—I needed time to think.'

'To think about what? Has he asked you to marry him?' Karen was eager now.

'Not in so many words, no. But I think he might.'

Karen raised her eyes heavenward. '*Glory!*'

Ashley twisted her hands together. 'Please—don't start making plans. I—I haven't made up my mind yet.'

'About what?'

'If—if he—if he should ask me to marry him. I—I don't know that I'd say yes.'

Karen got to her feet. 'For heaven's sake, why? You've said you think you love him. What more is there?'

'Karen, our lives are so different—have always been so different. I—the night we went out with—with Jake and Barbara—Mark and I, I mean. We went to this hotel——'

'I know. Mark told us all about it.'

'Yes, well, did he also tell you about Barbara meeting those friends of hers and Jake's? I admit, Jake wasn't enthusiastic about joining them, but Barbara insisted for a while. Well, I thought then that they were all alike—rich, experienced, sophisticated! I'm not like that. I don't want to be like that. I want to be me! I might even want to go on working after I was married. I'm not a socialite—I've no desire to be one. And—and besides, I doubt very much whether his family would be too pleased——'

'His family have nothing to do with it. You'd be marrying Jake, not his family.' Karen looked stunned. 'I just can't believe it. And I certainly can't believe that you—well, that you'd turn him down.'

'Wouldn't you?'

'Heavens, no!'

'Even if you didn't love him?'

'Ashley, you're forgetting something. Money!'

'No, I'm not. In fact, that's the whole problem, isn't it?'

'I don't believe it!' Karen stared at her in frustration. 'I really don't believe it. I've never met anyone like you before!'

Ashley made an awkward little gesture. 'Don't be silly!'

'It's true. I didn't know principles still existed in this hard and materialistic world of ours!'

'You're mocking me.'

'I'm not. I mean it. You flabbergast me, Ashley, you really do. Imagine having the chance to marry Jake Seton and turning it down!'

'I haven't been asked yet. And I'm still not sure what I'd do if I was,' declared Ashley unsteadily. 'There are too many things to consider. In some ways he's—well, he's been spoilt by the amount of attention he's always received. I think he likes to get his own way. I think he usually does.'

'I'm sure of it,' said Karen, with feeling. 'Dear me, just think—my little cousin might be the next Lady Seton!'

'Oh, don't!' A shadow crossed Ashley's face and Karen put her arm round the other girl's shoulders.

'All right, I won't say any more. But you'll have to have

some sort of an explanation for Mum. You got away with it very nicely just now—being sick and all. But she's bound to wonder where you disappeared to for the best part of two hours. She was very worried about you, you know.'

Ashley nodded. 'I'm sorry.'

'Well, who was this friend Jake took you to see? Couldn't you say you were there?'

Ashley's eyes brightened. 'Yes. Yes, of course. It was someone called Pearson—Joe Pearson——'

'The Setons' gamekeeper.'

'That's right. Do you know him?'

'Vaguely. I know *of* him. It figures that Jake would take you there, though. The old man's been like a father to him, so Mark says.'

'Their relationship did seem very close.'

'Hmm,' Karen nodded. 'So that's your excuse. And quite honestly, Mum being Mum, and thinking so kindly of Jake as she does, isn't likely to suspect that he's been—well, trying to make her ewe lamb!'

'Karen, that sounds horrible!'

'I could have used a more intimate word,' commented Karen dryly. 'And really, it can't have been his conversation that upset your nervous system to that extent.' She smiled wryly. 'I bet he's pretty good, isn't he? We must exchange confidences some time.'

Ashley managed a faint smile, but she knew that the last thing she would ever do was to tell someone else of her experiences with Jake. It was just not possible to share such intimacies with anyone other than Jake himself.

Even so, after the way he had stalked off earlier this evening, there was every chance that it might be some time before she saw him again, and this knowledge must not be allowed to tear her apart.

CHAPTER EIGHT

AUNT MONA was surprised but not overly distressed to learn that Jake had met Ashley accidentally outside the library and had offered to take her with him to visit the old gamekeeper. Ashley couldn't pretend she liked the deceit, but were she to attempt to explain what had really happened, her aunt would be even more shocked than Karen had been. So she apologised for not being able to enjoy the meal her aunt had prepared for her and made some excuse about eating something that didn't agree with her at Joe Pearson's. The incident passed over, and she breathed a sigh of relief when Aunt Mona looked at the clock and said she would have to hurry as she had promised to go to a whist drive with a friend of hers.

Ashley went into the lounge. Mark and Karen were there, and so was Jeff Saunders. They sat casually round the fire talking about the latest group to hit the pop scene, and during the conversation Ashley discovered that Jeff played the guitar. Mark laughed and said that one evening Jeff must bring the instrument round and play for them.

Knowing how shy Jeff was reputed to be, Ashley doubted he would do this, but she was glad that at last Karen seemed to have found herself a boy-friend who was intelligent as well as attractive. She half wished that Jake had been more like Jeff—financially at least. But then she squashed the thought. Jake was Jake—and if she loved him she would have to accept that. Accept his faults as well as his virtues—his weaknesses as well as his strength. It was because he was the man he was that she loved him, and while Jeff was good company, he didn't generate the kind of excitement that was always present when Jake was around.

She was not aware that Mark was speaking to her, and gave an apologetic little smile when he reached across and snapped his fingers just under her nose.

'I was asking whether Jake said anything about coming

down tonight. Karen says you saw him this afternoon.'

Ashley maintained her composure with an immense effort of self-will. 'Why, no. Were—were you expecting him?'

Mark shrugged. 'I thought he might call in,' he admitted. 'But I expect he has other commitments. After all, if he was out alone this afternoon, no doubt Barbara has insisted on his company this evening.'

Until that moment Ashley had given little thought to what Jake might be doing that evening, but now it troubled her. Where was he likely to be? With Barbara? Even if their engagement was broken, were they still seeing one another? She was a friend of the family as well as his ex-fiancée. And he had two sisters who probably liked her very much.

A stab of what she recognised was jealousy, pure and simple, caused a pain like a knife in her stomach. What if there was someone else—someone other than Barbara? A man like him was bound to have plenty of admirers—women such as he had spoken about—women who saw no shame in enjoying a man's company for its own sake—enjoying other, more intimate pleasures...

Her nails bit into her palms. She was being incredibly foolish thinking such thoughts. She had no hold on Jake Seton, just as he had no hold on her, and what he did with his time was his own affair. But all the same, the mere idea of him with another woman was sufficient to show her that she was not so much in control of her emotions as she would like to think she was.

Mark got to his feet. 'Let's have a drink,' he suggested, and Ashley said she would help him get them, glad of the chance to put her own personal anxieties to the back of her mind. Her uncle was in the bar as usual, and when he saw Ashley he came to the hall door, and said:

'Just the person I want to see. Get me a dozen tonics, will you, love? I think they'll see me through the rest of the evening.'

Ashley nodded, and went to get the bottles from the storeroom at the back of the hotel. When she came back she entered the bar behind the counter, and was about to bend and put them on the shelf when she saw Jake, seated at the bar, a glass of whisky between his fingers.

Her immediate instincts were to ignore him and escape from his sight as quickly as she could. She had changed while she was upstairs into her usual attire of sweater and shabby jeans, and her hair was tied back with a black ribbon. She felt drab and unsophisticated compared to his lean elegance and she stood staring at him, unable to think of anything to say.

He studied her with his usual intent gaze, but his expression was unreadable. However, he inclined his head and said: 'Hello, Ashley.'

'H-hello!' She was breathless, and she'd done nothing.

Her uncle looked round. 'Oh, there you are, Ashley. Put them down, girl. Or have you suddenly been paralysed?'

Ashley flushed. 'No, of course not.' She bent and thrust the bottles on to their shelf. 'Is—is that all you need?'

'I think so.' David was looking at her strangely. 'Is something wrong?'

'No.'

She shook her head and turned to go, and as she did so, Jake said: 'Can I see you for a moment, Ashley?'

She half turned, looking awkwardly towards her uncle. 'I—I suppose so. Do you—want to come round?'

David regarded them both frowningly and then with a shrug he bent and unfastened the gate and lifted that section of the bar which gave access to the room beyond. 'You'd better come this way,' he commented dryly, and Jake slid off his stool and walked through.

Ashley led the way into the hall, and then halted uncertainly. Jake was looking particularly disturbing this evening. He was wearing a velvet suit in a particularly attractive shade of dark blue, and the front of his white shirt was a mass of fine lace. She had never seen a man in a velvet suit before, and if anyone else had mentioned such a thing she would no doubt have considered it rather effeminate. But there was nothing effeminate about Jake, and it made her even more conscious of her own appearance.

'Well?' she began nervously. 'What—what do you want?'

Jake looked down at her silently for a long minute and

then he reached for her, drawing her determinedly towards him, curving her body into his. 'This——' he groaned thickly, and then his mouth was on hers and she ceased to think of anything else but him.

'I had to come back,' he muttered, against her neck. 'I didn't intend to. Not tonight. I was going to teach you a lesson by staying away. But you're under my skin—I can't keep away from you——'

Ashley felt a sensuous weakness as the soft velvet of his jacket rubbed against her midriff bared where her sweater had parted from her jeans. The fine material was like a caress against her skin. She could feel every hard muscle of his thighs through its yielding texture.

'Oh, Jake, I'm glad you did,' she breathed against his mouth, and then started as she heard Mark's voice. He was coming out of the lounge in search of her and unwillingly she dragged herself away from Jake, smoothing her sweater with trembling fingers.

Mark came out of the lounge looking impatient, but his expression changed when he saw Jake leaning negligently against the wall by the bar door.

'Hey, Jake!' he exclaimed, with obvious pleasure in his voice. 'Ashley, why didn't you ask Jake in? Come on, man. We're just having a drink. You can join us.'

Jake looked wryly at Ashley and then straightened. 'I didn't intend inviting myself in,' he remarked. 'Are you sure I'm not intruding?'

'Of course not.' Mark threw open the lounge door. 'Coming, Ashley?'

Ashley hesitated. She was aware that Jake was watching her closely and wondered whether he was angry with her for behaving so guiltily when Mark appeared. But quite honestly, it had been an involuntary reaction and now she half wished she had stayed where she was and let everyone find out how she felt about him.

She nodded her head in answer to Mark's query and with her head down walked ahead of them into the lounge. She heard Karen's swiftly indrawn breath when she saw who was following her, and seated herself on the small two-seater couch to one side of the fire where she and Mark had

110

been sitting earlier. But now it was Jake who came to share it with her, close beside her, smiling at her cousin.

'What'll you have, Jake?' Mark had a tray of bottles and glasses. 'I can offer you gin, whisky or lager.'

'A lager will do fine.' Jake relaxed against the stiff upholstery, one arm resting lazily along the back of Ashley's seat. 'Hmm, this is nice. Not going out tonight, Karen?'

'No.' Karen was brief.

Jake inclined his head. 'I don't blame you. It's started to rain.' He turned his attention to Jeff. 'By the way, did you get planning permission for those extensions?'

Jeff leaned forward. 'As a matter of fact, no.'

'Why not?'

'I believe there was some talk about a light obstruction.'

'Behind the shop?' Jake shook his head. 'That should be no problem.'

'I understand it was Mr. Ferris who objected.'

'Who? Graham Ferris?' Jake frowned. 'Is that official?'

Jeff sighed. 'More or less.'

Jake considered the toe of his suede boot. 'I'll have a word with my father. I can see no reason why permission shouldn't be granted.'

'I say, will you?' Jeff flushed. 'That's awfully good of you. I'd be very grateful.'

Jake shook his head and turned to look at Ashley. 'All right?' he asked softly, and she nodded, warmth welling up inside her at the look in his eyes. He picked up a strand of her hair and threaded it through his fingers. 'What would you call this?' he mused, apparently uncaring that Jeff and Karen were both watching him in astonishment. 'Blonde? Gold?'

'Does it matter?' Ashley was embarrassed.

'It might. If someone had to do a description of you.'

'Well, it doesn't come out of a bottle, if that's what you're wondering,' she declared quietly.

'I know that.' He smiled into her eyes and then allowed his gaze to linger a while on her mouth. It was an almost tangible contact, and when his arm dropped about her shoulders, drawing her closer to him, she did not resist. Her fingers lingered against the fine lace of his shirt front and he looked down at them and then into her eyes again. It was a deliberately sensual message that passed between them and Ashley had to draw away from him before the desire to reach up and pull his head down to hers overcame everything else.

Unfortunately Mark chose that moment to come towards them with their drinks, and he stopped short when he saw Jake's arm around Ashley's shoulders, and her hair gleaming softly against the dark blue velvet of his jacket.

Speaking more loudly than was necessary, he said: 'Here you are—here are your drinks. A lager and a tomato juice.'

Jake released Ashley to take their two glasses, grimacing as he handed her the thick red liquid. 'Tomato juice!' he exclaimed, with feeling. 'Don't you want anything stronger?'

'Ashley's only seventeen,' stated Mark, with more aggression than Ashley had ever known him display.

'I am aware of that.' Jake's tone was mild. He took a mouthful of his lager, apparently unperturbed by Mark's attitude. 'But she'll be eighteen next Tuesday.'

'How do you know?' It was Karen who voiced the question that trembled on Ashley's lips.

'My father is—as I'm sure you know—a member of the Council. He had to see the applications for the post at the library. I looked at his files.'

'The devil you did!' Mark looked annoyed. He was obviously finding it very difficult controlling his feelings, and right now Ashley sensed he needed some sort of an explanation.

Jake swallowed half of his lager, and then he too seemed to sense Mark's antipathy. Looking up, he said: 'Aren't you going to sit down, man? Or have I taken your seat?'

'As a matter of fact you have.' Mark was coldly brusque. 'But don't get up——' This as Jake was about to rise from the couch. 'After you've finished your lager, I'd like to have a word with you. Outside, if I may.'

Ashley felt terrible. 'Really, Mark——' she began, but Jake silenced her with a slight shake of his head.

'Sit down Mark, for goodness' sake.' Karen spoke impatiently. 'What's the matter with you?'

Mark clenched his fists, making no attempt to drink the glass of lager he had poured for himself. 'This is between Jake and me, Karen. You mind your own business.'

'I won't.' Karen looked angrily at him. 'You're making a fool of yourself. If you're annoyed because Jake had his arm around Ashley, don't be. Can't you see—she likes it!'

'What the hell is that supposed to mean?'

'Karen, please——'

Ashley tried to stop them, but it was Jake who rose to his feet, finishing his lager, and wiping his mouth with the back of his hand.

'All right, Mark,' he said pleasantly. 'I'm ready.'

'Jake——'

Ashley's voice was horrified, but he turned and made a calming movement with his hands before following Mark out of the door and into the hall.

The door closed behind them and Karen breathed a sigh of relief, but Ashley couldn't sit still. She rose restlessly to her feet and walked across the room, hesitating near the door and then turning back to the fire again.

'Relax.' Karen sounded resigned now. 'Mark's no good with his fists, and I'd back Jake against him any time.'

'You don't think—you don't think——'

'—that they're fighting? No. Oh, I think Mark might have taken his chances with another man if he thought you were being fooled, but Jake——' She shook her head. 'That's why he was so angry, I suppose. Because he thinks a lot of Jake, and he'd hate to lose his friendship.'

'So what do you think they're doing?' Ashley pressed her fingertips to her lips.

'I should think Jake is putting him straight, wouldn't you?' Karen frowned. 'I must admit I had my doubts about him, even after all you told me—but now...' She gave Jeff a helpless smile. 'What do you think?'

Jeff pursed his lips. 'I don't think it's for me to make any comment,' he said politely.

Karen wrinkled her nose at him. 'Politician! Still, it was kind of him to offer to speak to his father about your extension.'

'Yes, it was.' Jeff nodded. 'He's really a very nice man.'

'Nice?' echoed Karen dryly. 'Yes, I suppose you would say *nice*. That's not the word I'd use.' She chuckled. 'Oh, Ashley, did you see Mark's face when he saw Jake's arm around you?'

Ashley didn't answer. She was too concerned with what was going on outside, and when the door suddenly opened again, she stepped forward eagerly, halting as her uncle came face to face with her.

'Oh, there you are, Ashley,' he said. 'Come and get me some more crisps, will you? I've never known a Wednesday night to be so busy, and the girls don't have time to get them.'

'All right.'

With an apologetic shrug towards Karen, Ashley accompanied him into the hall, glancing round apprehensively, expecting to see Jake and Mark at one another's throats.

But they were not about, and she was forced to go and get the boxes of crisps that David wanted from the store-room. When she came back there was still no sign of them and she went into the lounge eagerly expecting to find them there, but as there was only Karen and Jeff, kissing in the corner, she came out again, quickly. Surely they couldn't be outside, she thought uneasily. Surely it hadn't come to that!

She went into the kitchen and waited, putting on the kettle and setting out cups on a tray for later. Aunt Mona always had a cup of cocoa before going to bed. Then she went back into the hall again and listened. But the only sound was the steady hum of noise from the bar.

She became really anxious, twisting her hands together, walking up and down. Where were they? What was going on? What had Jake said to him? And what had been Mark's reaction?

She was as jumpy as a cat and when the outer door opened she swung round in alarm, only to relax into nervous weakness as she saw Jake's lean features. Ignoring the man behind him, she rushed towards him, saying: 'Where have you been? What have you been doing? I've been so worried!'

Jake put his hands on her waist, holding her in front of

114

him but apart from him. 'Calm down,' he advised lazily, a smile touching the corners of his mouth. 'We've only been in the bar having a drink together.'

Ashley's gaze moved to Mark and she saw a rather sheepish expression in his face. 'That's right, Ashley,' he said, thrusting his hands into his trousers pockets. 'I'm sorry. I behaved like a boor. I—I never imagined...'

Jake shook his head. 'No sweat,' he commented quietly. 'Look, honey, I've got to go. It's late—after ten. And you've got school tomorrow.'

Ashley's lips drooped. 'It's early,' she protested.

'You know you're not usually late to bed when it's school tomorrow,' said Mark.

Ashley gave him an impatient look. 'Since when have you made yourself responsible for my welfare!' she flared.

Mark flushed. 'I'm not making myself responsible for your welfare. You know I'm right.'

Ashley turned back to Jake, wishing he would stop holding her away from him. She badly wanted to feel his hard body against hers. She wished Mark would just go away and leave them alone.

But he didn't, and Jake released her before turning towards the door. 'I'll see you tomorrow,' he said softly, and she nodded, conscious of a lump in her throat. She had to stand there while the door closed behind him and then she marched mutinously towards the stairs, fighting back the tears that trembled on the brink of her eyes.

'Goodnight, Ashley.' Mark had followed her and was waiting for her to go upstairs before going back into the lounge.

Ashley took several stairs and then turned to glare down at him. 'What did you say to him?' she demanded hotly.

Mark frowned. 'Why, nothing much.'

'Then what did he say to you?'

'He told me that he and Barbara have—split up. That the engagement's off, for the moment——'

'*For the moment?*'

Ashley sounded horrified, and Mark hastened on: 'Well, I admit he didn't actually say that. Not in so many words. But it's always possible that it is only a temporary thing, isn't it? I mean, he and Barbara have known one another for such a long time. It's conceivable that they need a break——'

'A break!' Ashley almost choked. 'Oh, Mark! Why can't you mind your own business, like Karen said!'

And with that she turned and ran headlong up the stairs, not stopping until the door of the room she shared with Karen had slammed behind her.

Inevitably, the following morning she felt terrible.

She had slept fitfully after taking four aspirins in an attempt to force sleep on herself before Karen could come to bed and start asking questions, and when she woke her head ached abominably.

Fortunately, Karen overslept, and the two girls were too busy getting ready for their individual occupations to find time for chatter. Mona, too, thought that Ashley's pallor was a hangover from her nausea of the night before, and didn't press her to eat a lot at breakfast.

The morning dragged before Miss Kincaid sent for her, and when she did Ashley went without enthusiasm to answer the summons. She knew the headmistress would not be keen on her settling for such a mundane post.

'You have an excellent brain, Ashley,' she said seriously. 'You could quite easily get a degree and take up some sort of university teaching yourself. Don't you want to use your abilities to their best advantage? I have teenagers here, boys as well as girls, who would give their eye teeth to have your opportunities, and here you are, throwing them away. There was never any doubt about your being accepted at the library. They have the sense to realise the advantages you are offering them.'

'You're very kind.'

'I'm not kind at all,' exclaimed Miss Kincaid. 'I'm simply being honest, that's all.' She walked across to the window of her study and looked out over the playing fields of the school. Then she turned and said: 'There is one more thing, Ashley.'

'Yes?' Ashley tipped her head on one side.

'It has to do with you—you personally.'

'Oh, yes?'

'Yes.' Miss Kincaid was obviously finding it difficult to put what she had to say into words. 'Ashley, this morning I was told that yesterday afternoon you were seen with Sir James Seton's son, outside the Golden Lion—your home, in fact.'

Ashley stiffened. She might have known Jake could not get away with something like that without their being observed. Folding her hands together in her lap, she said: 'Yes, that's right.'

Miss Kincaid's brows drew together. 'There was more,' she continued dryly. 'I was told—you were kissing. Was that an exaggeration? I sincerely hope it was. I've always considered you a sane and sensible girl, Ashley, not given to irresponsible behaviour—like getting involved with a man, many years your senior, and one moreover who is already engaged to somebody else.'

Ashley looked down at her hands. 'I'd rather not talk about it, if you don't mind.'

Miss Kincaid clicked her tongue. She was a woman in her forties, tall and angular, the epitome of the school-marmish spinster characterised in so many novels and so rare to find today, and all her life she had striven to instil a sense of knowledge into minds brainwashed by pop music and television. But in Ashley she had sensed something else —a sensitivity—an intelligence that had endeared itself to her. She liked Ashley, she wanted her to do well, and in her view the girl was throwing herself away in a dead-end job because she was infatuated by a man who would be married to someone else before the summer was over. Everything inside her recoiled from such a relationship. She had never been involved with a man, and while she would not wish her unmarried state on anyone she had hoped that Ashley would make a success of her career before settling down to marriage.

'Very well,' she said now. 'I can't force you.'

Ashley rose to her feet. 'May I go?'

Miss Kincaid sighed. 'I suppose so. But do think about this carefully, Ashley. Don't do anything your father would not have wished you to do.'

117

Ashley thought over what the headmistress had said as she ate lunch in the canteen with Susan Knight. In one way, Miss Kincaid was right. Her father would have wanted her to go to university, but that was because he had had little time for her himself, and she had felt happiest in an academic background, immersed in her books.

Now it was different. Now she had a home, a real home for the first time since she was a child, and she didn't want to give it up for the loneliness and austerity of a bedsitter in some distant place of learning.

She noticed Susan was looking rather morose too, and pushing her own troubles aside, she said: 'What's wrong, Sue? Had a row with Barry?'

Barry Lester was Susan's current boy-friend, a boy in their year, who was hoping to become an engineer when he had completed his 'A' levels.

Susan shook her head and pushed her plate aside. 'Actually, no.' She paused. 'Ashley, there's a rumour going round that you—that you're involved with Jake Seton. Is it true?'

Ashley flushed. 'Oh, Susan,' she murmured unhappily.

'Why didn't you tell me?' Susan sounded hurt. 'We've never had any secrets from each other, have we? I mean, I've told you all about Barry, haven't I?'

Ashley sighed. 'I—I couldn't discuss it with anyone. Besides, I don't even know what there is to discuss.'

Susan gave her an impatient look. 'Well, do be careful. I've lived in Bewford longer than you have, and I know Jake Seton. He'll marry Barbara St. John Forrest and you'll be left high and dry, no matter what he tells you. Heavens, they've been together for years. The only amazing thing is that they haven't got married before this. Still——' She gave Ashley an old-fashioned look, 'I don't suppose marriage will make much difference to their relationship, if you see what I mean.'

Ashley looked down at her plate. 'I can guess.'

'Well! It's obvious, isn't it?' She wrinkled her nose at the dish of watery macaroni in front of her. 'By the way, did you see the picture of them in this morning's *Echo*?'

Ashley's head jerked up. 'P-Picture of who?' she stammered.

'Jake Seton and Barbara St. John Forrest.'

Ashley shook her head, trying to clear the confusion from her brain. Jake had been at the Golden Lion last night . . .

Yes, a voice inside her mocked. *But he left very early, didn't he?*

She forced herself to speak calmly. 'I—I slept in this morning. What picture? Wh-where were they?'

Susan frowned. 'It was one of those Rotary Club affairs. At the Carlton Arms.'

'But when was the picture taken?' Ashley insisted unsteadily.

Susan looked at her with concern. 'What's wrong? You're looking awfully pale. Are you all right?'

'Yes, yes, I'm perfectly all right. When was the picture taken?'

'Well, last night, I suppose. It's usually the previous day's events that are reported, isn't it?' She hesitated. 'Ashley, what's wrong? You look ghastly.'

'And you say—they were together?'

'Who? Jake and Barbara? Well, they were on the same photograph. I don't know whether they were together or not. He didn't have his arms around her or anything.'

'I see.' Ashley swallowed hard. She pushed her plate aside. She hadn't had much appetite to begin with. Now she felt positively sick at the thought of food.

Fortunately soon afterwards they were joined by Barry Lester and a few of his friends and Ashley's silence was not so noticeable. She managed to smile in the right places and was inordinately relieved when the bell for the end of the lunch break was rung.

However, as she and Susan left the school that evening, she saw the sleek green Ferrari parked just outside the gates and her heart began to pound so loudly she was amazed that Susan couldn't hear it.

'He's waiting for you, I suppose,' Susan observed dryly.

'Yes. Yes, I suppose so.' Ashley's mouth felt parched. They had reached the school gates now and her instincts were to turn and go back into the school. Anything to avoid talking to him after what she had learned at lunchtime.

But of course she had to go on. The sleek saloon was

attracting a great deal of attention, particularly from the boys, and she wondered how he dared to come here knowing the kind of speculation his presence would cause.

Susan patted her shoulder. 'See you tomorrow,' she said significantly, and walked away.

Ashley nodded. There was no avoiding him now and she was as nervous as a kitten. She hesitated uncertainly by the gates. What if for some reason best known to himself he had not come to meet her? How could she walk over to the car and ask him what he was doing?

Her dilemma was resolved, however, when the door of the car was thrust open and Jake got half out, beckoning to her. She walked towards him and he said: 'Hello,' before getting inside again and sliding across into his own seat. 'Had a good day?'

Ashley glanced round, conscious of being the cynosure of all eyes as she levered herself into the low squab seat and slammed the door behind her. Then she glanced across at him. 'It was all right,' she replied politely.

Jake leant forward and started the engine, pulling away with his usual surge of speed. Then he looked back over his shoulder and said: 'That should provide a common topic of conversation for afternoon tea, shouldn't it?'

Ashley looked out of the windows at the swiftly passing houses. 'You shouldn't have such a conspicuous vehicle if you don't want to be recognised.'

'Did I say I didn't want to be recognised?' he enquired, his tone mildly rebuking.

'No, but ...' She sighed. 'Have you had a good day?'

'I've had a busy day. I just got back from Leeds half an hour ago.'

'Leeds?' Ashley was momentarily diverted. 'On business?'

She asked the question innocently enough, but then could have bitten out her tongue for being curious. After all, the Setons' private business was nothing to do with her. But Jake didn't seem to take it that way.

'We own some land, over towards High Ingram—where the old sawmill used to be. My father wants to sell it—for development. There's been some difficulties concerning the

120

tenants' rights, and I've been trying to iron them out. I think it's going to be pretty straightforward from now on.'

Ashley bit her lip. They had almost reached the Golden Lion. 'I'm sorry,' she said awkwardly. 'I mean—well, it's nothing to do with me. I didn't mean to be inquisitive.'

Jake gave her an impatient look. 'Don't be silly,' he said, and his tone was definitely reproving now. 'You have every right to ask a perfectly innocent question. Besides, I thought it might be of interest to you.'

'It was. It is.'

The car was drawing to a halt outside the hotel and Ashley wished desperately that she was not always so edgy where he was concerned. But he had said nothing about the night before and she could not ask. What was he thinking? Why had he come to meet her? She should have asked.

The car stopped and she gathered her belongings together in her lap. 'Thank you,' she said stiffly. 'It—it was kind of you to meet me.'

'Is that all you have to say?'

'Well—well, what else is there? I mean, was there some reason why you came to meet me? Something you wanted to—to tell me?'

Jake half turned in his seat towards her. 'There was a reason, yes.'

Ashley's heart plunged. Had he come to tell her that he and Barbara had made it up? That their engagement was valid again? She wondered with a sense of desperation how she would bear such a thing.

But Jake didn't seem tense. On the contrary he was lazily relaxed as he said: 'I have an invitation for you. From my mother.'

'Your mother!' Ashley was astounded.

'That's right. It's a perfectly normal development. My parents—my family—want to meet you. That's natural enough, isn't it?'

'Is it?' Ashley moved her shoulders in a confused gesture.

'Of course it is.' Jake swung round in his seat, tapping his fingers impatiently against the steering wheel. 'Ashley, what is it with you? The minute I leave you, you seem to

121

change. Last night—well, last night I thought we understood one another——'

Ashley reached for the door handle, but he was quicker than she was, capturing her hands in his and preventing her escape effortlessly. He was closer now than he had been before, and his warm breath fanned her cheek.

'Well?' he challenged. 'I'm right, aren't I? Something's wrong. Somebody's said something or done something, and you've decided that I have nothing to say in the matter.' He looked down at her mouth, his own frankly sensuous. 'Ashley, what is it you want me to say? That I love you? I do. That I need you? I do. That I want you? *God*—do you doubt it?'

Ashley drew a trembling breath. 'You were with Barbara last night,' she accused unevenly.

Jake stared at her, his eyes narrowing disbelievingly. 'Who told you that?'

'I didn't have to be told, did I? There's a picture of you together in this morning's *Echo*! No wonder you looked so—so—well, no wonder you were wearing that beautiful suit! It wasn't for my benefit, was it? It was for some—some Rotary affair!'

Jake studied her unhappy face for a long moment, then he raised one of her hands to his lips. 'Oh, Ashley,' he said, shaking his head. 'Do you have so little faith in me?'

Ashley's lids flickered upward and she looked into his eyes. 'Were you there?'

'At the Rotary dinner-dance—yes. I went there after leaving the hotel.'

'Oh!' She struggled to take her fingers from his, but he wouldn't let her.

'What's wrong with that? I was supposed to be there at eight o'clock. As it was I arrived about ten-thirty.'

'With Barbara?'

'No, not with Barbara. Though why I should have to say that, I can't imagine.' He shook his head. 'Ashley, I've told you. Barbara and I are finished. She knows that as well as I do. It's only a matter of time before the news is made public.'

'But—but——'

'Look, these Rotary affairs are local events. The Forrests as well as the Setons are expected to put in an appearance. If the photographer happened to take a picture that included both of us, that's not my fault, is it?'

'But why didn't you tell me that you were going?'

'I didn't intend to go,' replied Jake quietly. 'But after talking with Mark——'

'Mark? What did he say?'

Jake shook his head. 'This and that.' He looked round impatiently at the milling shoppers thronging the street. 'Ashley, you will come to dinner tomorrow evening, won't you? My mother is expecting you.'

'Tomorrow evening?'

Jake sighed. 'Yes. I can't see you tonight. I have to speak to Warren Forrest about the development plans.'

'Warren Forrest? Is he—is he some relation——'

'He's Barbara's father, yes. And no doubt I'll see Barbara, too. But I shan't touch her, if that's what's worrying you.'

'She might—she might make the—the advances.'

Jake's expression was wry. 'I think Barbara and I understand one another in that direction.'

'Was she—I mean——' Ashley's cheeks burned. 'Was she your—your mistress?' There, it was out, and she dared not look at him.

He considered her downbent head for a moment and then he tilted her chin upward. 'Yes,' he said, honestly, 'she was. But since I met you I've never even looked at another woman, let alone anything else.'

Ashley felt an overwhelming sense of longing for him. She badly wanted to show him how she felt, and on impulse she leant towards him and pressed a swift kiss to the corner of his mouth, putting her hand behind his head to hold him closer for a moment. Then she turned and thrust open her door, climbing out before she felt compelled to do something even more reckless.

Jake got out more leisurely, slamming his door and nodding in acknowledgement of a greeting called to him from across the street. He came round to Ashley's side and took a firm grip on her wrist.

'Tomorrow—yes?'

'Wh-what time?'

'I'll pick you up here at seven. We usually have drinks before dinner. It will give you an opportunity to meet my parents and my sisters before we eat.'

Ashley nodded. 'All right. But what do I wear?'

Jake smiled gently. 'Nothing formal. A dress—a suit. A trouser suit, if you'd rather. I don't care what you wear. You look beautiful in anything.'

Ashley's lips tilted. 'Thank you.' She glanced over her shoulder. 'I should go in now. I don't want to alarm Aunt Mona a second time.' She bent her head. 'Think of me—tonight!'

Jake looked round them and then with an impatient movement urged her ahead of him up the cobbled yard at the side of the hotel. Once they were out of sight of the road, he pulled her into his arms and possessed her mouth with almost desperate hunger.

'There,' he said at last, pushing her away, his mouth strained. 'Does that reassure you?'

Ashley nodded tremulously, and after giving her another devastating look he turned and left her.

CHAPTER NINE

OVER their meal that evening, Ashley told her aunt and uncle of her dinner invitation.

Her aunt was obviously flabbergasted and stared at her in amazement. 'But why?' she exclaimed, at last. 'Is Mark invited as well?'

'No.' Ashley shook her head.

'This has to do with Jake coming here yesterday evening, hasn't it?' her uncle said perceptively.

Ashley nodded.

'So what's going on? Jake's marrying that Forrest girl. I won't have him messing around with you!'

Ashley sighed. 'He's broken the engagement.'

'What?' Her aunt looked even more astounded. 'But why? Not—not because of you? Oh, Ashley, you're not—you're not in trouble, are you?'

Ashley had to smile then. 'No, Aunt Mona, I'm not pregnant, if that's what you're afraid of.'

'Then what's going on?' Mona pushed her plate of steak and salad aside. 'You've quite put me off my tea. I think you'd better explain. From the beginning.'

'Now, Mona . . .' Her husband gave her a reproving look.

'Well,' she cried defensively, 'I knew nothing about it.'

'I don't mind telling you,' exclaimed Ashley, cupping her chin on her fists. 'I—we——' She paused, searching for the right words. 'We were attracted to one another—from the beginning, I think. Now—now I think I'm in love with him.'

'What about him?' demanded her aunt. 'Is he in love with you?'

'He says he is——'

'And you believe him?'

'Mona!' David spoke impatiently. 'Give the girl a chance!'

'Well, I've never heard anything like it! Sir James

Seton's only son and—and my niece! It doesn't sound possible! Ashley, are you sure there's not more to this than you're admitting?'

Ashley felt her face going red. 'No. *No!* Aunt Mona, I wouldn't lie to you. I—I—I've never——'

'Of course you haven't.' Her uncle put a reassuring hand on her wrist. 'Your aunt's shocked, that's all.' He shook his head. 'We both are. But I did see the way he was looking at you last night, and—well, I have heard a rumour——'

'But you never said a word!' Mona accused him hotly.

'I would have done—if I'd thought it was the truth.'

'Well? What was it?'

'Just that Jake and Barbara were—well—splitting up.'

'I don't believe it.' Mona got up abruptly from the table. 'I *can't* believe it. Why, they've been going together for years——'

'Too many years,' commented her husband dryly. 'Don't you know what they say about familiarity?'

'I know, but—but Ashley!' She turned to look at the girl. 'Don't you find it all—rather overwhelming?'

Ashley bent her head. 'Of course I do.'

'And has he asked you to marry him, then?'

'No. No, he hasn't.'

'Is he going to?'

'I don't know.' Ashley looked up helplessly. 'Aunt Mona, it's only a dinner invitation, not a declaration of intent.'

David nodded vigorously. 'Yes, that's right. We're making far too much fuss about it. For heaven's sake, Mona, leave the girl alone!'

Mona gave him a killing look and then went to carry the teapot to the table. As she poured out cups of the steaming beverage, she said: 'And you kept all this to yourself. Didn't you think we had a right to know what was going on?'

'Ashley bit her lip unhappily. 'Of course I did. But I—I didn't know myself, not really—until yesterday.'

'Of course!' Mona plumped down into her seat. 'Of course, Jake met you from the library, didn't he?' She shook her head. 'And that was when he told you he'd broken his engagement?'

126

'Yes', Ashley nodded, stirring her tea.

'Imagine it!' Mona couldn't leave it alone, in spite of her husband's warning glances. 'Our niece—and Sir James Seton's son!' She shook her head. 'I'd like to see Lady Seton's face when she has to greet us as her son's in-laws!'

'Aunt Mona. please!' Ashley's hands were clenched. 'You're anticipating too much.' She sighed. 'Even if—even if Jake should ask me to—well, marry him, I—I don't know whether—whether I should accept.'

Mona was in the middle of taking a mouthful of tea and she choked on it, gasping: '*What?*'

'You heard the girl,' declared her husband sharply. 'Now leave her alone!'

'But, Ashley——' Her aunt gulped and wiped her mouth with her handkerchief. 'Ashley, whatever are you saying?'

'There's a great gulf between Jake and me,' explained Ashley carefully. 'His way of life and mine are totally different——'

'Not *so* different!'

'Totally different,' insisted Ashley quietly. 'I realise that. The women he knows have always been used to plenty of money—a certain standard of living. They're quite happy just being decorative. They play golf, I suppose—do charitable works.' She shrugged. 'I don't honesly know how they fill their time. But I don't think I should like it. I have a brain—I want to use it, not become a—a cabbage!'

'A cabbage!' Her aunt was shocked. 'Ashley!—What a thing to say.'

'Well, I can't help it.'

'But what about a home—a family? You want children, don't you?'

Children!

The idea was intoxicating. There was something deeply disturbing about imagining herself bearing Jake's children, but she pushed temptation aside. There was more to marriage than having children.

'Of course I want children,' she said now. 'But—oh, Aunt Mona, try to understand how I feel! I don't want Jake to marry me just to provide an heir for the Setons! I want him to respect me, to respect my ideals—my opinions! I should want some sort of freedom when it came to running our home, and I certainly shouldn't want half a dozen servants running after my every wish!'

Mona shook her head disbelievingly. 'I don't believe it. I thought I'd heard everything, but I hadn't. Imagine considering turning down marrying Jake Seton! It doesn't bear thinking about.'

'Mona, please! Leave the girl alone!' David sounded angry. 'She knows her own mind best.' He studied his niece thoughtfully. 'It seems to me that Jake knows what he's doing. After the women he's used to associating with, you must be a refreshing diversion. I wonder if he realises exactly what he's letting himself in for.'

Ashley felt the corners of her mouth twitching. Uncle David was always so calm, so reassuring. He reduced everything to practicalities and she was grateful to him for his good sense.

However, the following evening no one could reassure her when it came to contemplating her coming confrontation with the Seton family. She had never met a titled person before, and she was afraid she would say all the wrong things and make an absolute fool of herself. How would Jake react if his family didn't like her? How would she react if she didn't like them? It was terrifying, and her hands were trembling as she applied a honey-coloured lipstick. What would she say to them? She wasn't any good at small talk. Apart from anything else, she wasn't used to it.

The bedroom door opened and Karen came into the room.

'He's here,' she announced blandly. 'Are you nearly ready?'

Ashley swung round, checking the front zipper of her pants. 'Don't I look as though I am?'

Karen frowned. 'You're wearing a slack suit?'

'Yes. Why? Don't you think I should?' Ashley was anxious.

Her cousin considered her appearance. 'Well, you suit trousers,' she admitted slowly. 'But isn't a suit a bit—ordinary?'

Ashley looked down at the cream flared pants with their matching back-vented jacket. 'Do you think so?' She touched the collar of the flame-coloured blouse she was wearing with them. 'I thought it looked quite—attractive.'

'It does. But I'd have thought that long black skirt that you wore before—and perhaps that blouse,' Karen sounded doubtful.

'Oh, Karen!' The last thing Ashley wanted was to have to worry about her appearance on top of everything else. 'I don't know what to think. Do you think both his sisters will be there?'

'It sounds possible, although Hilary, she's the younger of the two, she's still at university.'

Ashley sighed. 'Karen, universities are finished for the Easter break!' She smoothed her hands down over her flat stomach. 'Do you realise I know nothing about his family except for what you've told me. What's his other sister called? And how old is she?'

'Jennifer? Oh, she must be twenty-four or five. They're both older than you are.'

'Then why aren't they married—or Jennifer, at least?'

'Don't say that,' warned Karen quickly. 'Jennifer was engaged about three years ago. Her fiancé was Malcolm Ainsley, the racing driver.'

'But wasn't he——' Ashley halted and nodded. 'He was killed, wasn't he?'

'That's right. Only six weeks before the wedding. I don't remember it myself. I mean I was only about fifteen or sixteen at that time. But Mum told me later on, when I started asking the same sort of questions as you've just asked.'

'Yes. It was in all the papers.' Ashley turned to give herself another dissatisfied appraisal. 'Lord, why did I ever agree to this? I—I don't even know why I'm going.'

'You're going to meet Jake's parents, aren't you? It happens in all the best families.'

Ashley grimaced. 'I know that. But—well, what's the point? Jake and I may never ...' She shrugged her slim shoulders. 'Why couldn't things just go on the way they were? Meeting his parents seems so—so formal, somehow.'

Karen gave her an exasperated look. 'You're making it that way. Gosh, I've met lots of boys' parents.'

'Have you?' Ashley sounded uncertain. 'But not in these circumstances, I suppose.'

'No. I'll admit no man has ever thrown over his fiancée for me!'

'Oh, Karen!'

'Stop worrying! Hell, if he looked at me like he looks at you, I shouldn't feel anxious about a little thing like meeting his parents.'

Downstairs, Ashley found Jake waiting in the lounge with her aunt and Mark. He looked relieved when he saw her, however, and she paused to wonder exactly what had been said. His eyes signified his approval of her appearance, and she felt a little of the tension go out of her. So long as he was satisfied, what else mattered?

'What time will you be home, Ashley?' Aunt Mona asked, as she accompanied them to the door.

Ashley felt uncomfortable. 'I'm not sure,' she said, looking to Jake for confirmation. 'But not late.'

'I should hope not.' Mona was reproving. 'After all, you're not used to late nights.'

Jake inclined his head good-humouredly. 'And I am,' he commented.

'Well, aren't you?'

'I guess so.' He pushed Ashley ahead of him out of the door. 'Don't worry—*Aunt* Mona, I shan't keep her out after midnight.'

Ignoring Mona's startled reaction, they walked down the cobbled yard to the street where the Ferrari was parked, and once inside Jake gave her another appraising stare. 'Very nice,' he remarked, leaning towards her and kissing her cheek. 'Hmm, you smell good. What is it?'

'Chanel. It's my birthday present from Mark. He gave it to me this evening—for this special occasion.'

'Some special occasion,' observed Jake dryly, starting the engine and leaving her to wonder exactly what he meant by that.

Bewford Hall was reached by a private road through the Bewford estate. The estate itself stretched to the outskirts

130

of town and as well as acres of moor, there were farms and smallholdings tenanted by the estate workers just as there had been two hundred years ago when the Hall was first built. The Hall was backed by a copse of pine trees and stood at the end of a long drive flanked by paddocks. It was an attractive Georgian house, and in the mellow light of an April evening was looking at its best. It was not as large as Ashley had imagined, but it was big enough to bring a surge of apprehension to her nervous system.

A grey Bentley was parked on the forecourt, and after observing Ashley's interest, Jake said: 'My father's,' in quiet tones.

He parked the Ferrari beside the other car, and then said, unnecessarily: 'Well, we're here!'

'Yes.' Ashley took a deep breath. 'Oh, Jake, I'm terrified!'

'Don't be.'

Jake opened his door and slid out, leaving her to do likewise, and she felt a sense of disappointment. Although he had seemed pleased to see her initially, since leaving town he had become silent and morose, and she wondered whether he was regretting bringing her here. What if he was ashamed of her—of her inexperience, her lack of sophistication? And apart from that cool kiss when they got into the car he had not even touched her.

Her door swung open and she looked up to find him holding it for her. She swung her legs round and stepped out, and he closed the door behind her. He was looking particularly dark and saturnine this evening in a dark blue lounge suit with a navy shirt and tie, and she thought how well the dark clothes suited his present mood.

They went up several shallow stone steps and Jake opened the white-painted door. They entered an attractive oak-panelled hall with a soft, amber-coloured carpet underfoot. A staircase, also panelled, led to the upper floors of the building, and Ashley could see a circular window illuminating the first landing. The house was warm from an efficient heating system, and there was a mixed but distinct aroma of Havana tobacco and beeswax.

As Jake closed the door behind them, a man of indeterminate age appeared through a door at the back of the hall and came to greet them. Ashley's nerves tautened. Who was this? Surely not Jake's father!

Jake allayed these fears by saying: 'Good evening, Barnes. Where are my parents?'

'Good evening, Master Jake.' Barnes' sharp eyes assessed Ashley very thoroughly. 'Sir James and Lady Seton are in the library, sir.'

'Thank you.'

Jake nodded a dismissal and putting his hand beneath Ashley's elbow led her across to another door, panelled in a darker oak, with a long gold handle. Ashley looked up at him once, but he didn't return her gaze. He merely pressed the handle, and the door swung open ahead of them.

Urged on by the hand at her elbow, Ashley was forced to enter the book-lined room which at first glance seemed filled with people. She trembled visibly and Jake's hand fell from her elbow as he moved to her side to perform the introductions.

The group of people resolved themselves into a middle-aged woman and a somewhat older man who must be Sir James and Lady Seton, Ashley decided. There were also a woman in her twenties, who might be Jennifer, a younger girl, who judging by her resemblance to Jake must be his youngest sister, Hilary, and a youngish man whose identity she could not begin to guess at. There was a definite air of antagonism in the room, and she had the feeling that their arrival had interrupted some argument which had been going on.

Jake took her first to his parents. Lady Seton was reclining gracefully on a low couch, and her husband was standing nearby, his back to the screen that concealed the empty firegrate. They were an imposing couple, but Ashley was relieved to see that neither of them were formally dressed.

Lady Seton however viewed her appearance with less than friendliness, which became obvious when she said: 'I understand you work in a public house, Miss Calder.'

Ashley forced herself not to retaliate. To reduce this first meeting to a verbal sparring contest was unthinkable, and her voice was cool and polite as she replied: 'No, Lady

Seton, my uncle and aunt keep a small hotel. I'm still at school.'

Sir James was less hostile. He gave her a thorough appraisal, and then said: 'You're the young lady who has recently been appointed to the new post at the library, aren't you? What are you doing taking up a position like that with the kind of qualifications you've got?'

Ashley's lips parted in surprise. Then she remembered what Jake had said. His father had had access to her application which had given a comprehensive account of her abilities to date.

'You mean why am I not going on to university, Sir James?'

He nodded.

'Well, until the end of last year I fully intended to do so. But my father died and I had to come north and live with my aunt and uncle. Since then, they've made me so welcome, I feel little desire to uproot myself again. I like living in Bewford——'

'What she means is—why should she work hard to achieve some small success for herself when Jake is apparently available!' drawled Hilary, from her position on the arm of her sister's chair. 'After all, everyone knows he's a much more desirable achievement!'

'*Hilary!*'

Her father spoke angrily, and although Ashley couldn't see Jake's face she knew he was angry, too. She herself felt terrible. She had expected nothing like this.

'Well, isn't it true?' demanded Hilary, refusing to be quelled. 'Anyone can see she's got an eye to the main chance——'

'*Leave the room!*'

Sir James's voice was no louder than before, but the message was only too clear.

'But, Daddy——' Hilary got reluctantly to her feet, standing there before him, slim and youthful in a plain navy skirt and red jumper, her hair straight and dark like Jake's. She must have been about two years older than Ashley, but she behaved much younger.

'Hilary, I will not have you speaking like that in front of

133

a guest in my house!' said her father grimly. 'Now, I will give you the opportunity to apologise at once or you may, as I have said, leave the room and have your dinner upstairs!'

'James, isn't that rather harsh——'

Lady Seton defended her younger daughter with an impatient frown, but her husband was not prepared to be lenient.

'Hilary knows better than that,' he replied coldly. 'Well, Hilary?'

Hilary pressed her lips together mutinously. Then she shrugged. 'All right, all right, I'm sorry.' Her gaze flickered over Ashley in a way that conveyed to the younger girl only too clearly that she was merely paying lip service to her father's dictum.

Jake, who had stood silently through this, now moved towards his other sister, introducing Ashley with cool indifference. But to Ashley's relief, Jennifer was in no way like her sister.

'Hello, Ashley,' she greeted her smilingly. 'You must be getting a terribly biased view of this family. Believe me, they're not half as bad as they seem.'

Ashley smiled. She thought she could like Jennifer, but at the moment she was hardly in a position to judge. In this hostile atmosphere any friendly face would appear as a lifeline.

The youngish man turned out to be Gerald Sawyer, a friend of Jennifer's. He was apparently a solicitor in Bewford, and his manner was that of an interested bystander and nothing more, much to Ashley's relief.

Everyone but Jake and Ashley already had a drink, and with what Ashley felt was an enforced show of geniality, Sir James asked her what she would like. She hesitated uncertainly, and was relieved when Jake said: 'I think a sherry would be suitable, Father.'

Sir James nodded. 'And you, of course, want Scotch.'

'If it's not too much trouble,' agreed Jake, his lips twisting rather mockingly, and Ashley saw his father respond to the gesture. It was obvious that whatever else was present in this room, Jake and his father shared a good relationship.

'Won't you sit down?'

That was Jennifer. She patted the chair beside hers and with a backward glance at Jake, Ashley went to take it. Right now, she had never felt so remote from him, and she wished he would look at her properly and show her that he had not suddenly become the stranger he appeared. He fitted into these surroundings. His clothes, his attitudes, everything about him had been influenced by his upbringing, while she felt hopelessly out of her depth.

'Tell me, Miss Calder, how long have you known my son?'

Ashley's head jerked up and she encountered Lady Seton's intent stare. 'Er—about six or seven weeks,' she answered awkwardly.

'Six or seven weeks,' echoed Lady Seton, inhaling with delicate precision. 'Not very long, you will agree.'

'It rather depends on the relationship, doesn't it, Mother?' Jennifer challenged, with a reassuring smile in Ashley's direction.

Lady Seton gave her elder daughter an impatient glance. 'I would accept that, Jennifer. Nevertheless, you have to admit, when compared to other—relationships, it is a very short time.'

Ashley wished Jake would say something. He had accompanied his father across the room to the drinks cabinet which stood in one corner and she could hear the low murmur of their voices in the background.

Now Jennifer said: 'If you're talking about Jake's association with Barbara, then of course I have to agree. But quite honestly, I always thought they were taking a little too long to get to the altar.'

Lady Seton ignored her daughter. 'You're only seventeen, aren't you, Miss Calder? Don't you think you're a little young to be—well, involved with a man so much older?'

Ashley sighed. 'I shall be eighteen in four days' time, Lady Seton. And I don't feel so much younger than Jake.'

Jake turned then and came towards her with a glass of sherry in his hands. He gave it to her and she looked up into his eyes appealingly. But he turned away, and a slow-burning flame of resentment sprang up inside her. How dared he bring her here and ignore her like this? Couldn't he hear what his mother was saying? Didn't he care?

'Nowadays men marry women young enough to be their daughters and no one takes the slightest notice,' remarked Jennifer mildly. 'Besides, looking at Ashley, I doubt very much whether Jake took her age into consideration, did you, Jake?'

Jake had taken a glass of Scotch from his father and was drinking it slowly, one hand thrust into the pocket of his jacket as he did so.

'I believe you're nine years younger than my father, aren't you, Mama?' he enquired lazily.

His mother frowned, running a smoothing hand over her immaculately styled hair. She must once have been as dark as her son, but now her hair was streaked with grey, albeit in a most attractive way.

'That was different, darling,' she insisted. 'Your father and I had known one another for several years before our marriage. Just as—just as you and Barbara——'

'I can't imagine why everyone is talking about marriage!' Ashley suddenly broke out jerkily, almost snapping the slender stem of her wine glass between her fingers. 'I don't want to get married for years yet!'

Dinner was served in an attractive room overlooking the gardens at the back of the house. It was getting dark by the time they all sat around the long table and the servants had lit two candelabra and placed them beside the bowl of tulips and narcissi which graced the centre of the table. Silver cutlery and cut glass reflected in the polished wood, while white napkins stood stiffly at every place.

Since Ashley's precipitate announcement the conversation had been stilted, but general, with Ashley herself taking very little part in it, and although she told herself she was relieved she knew she was not. One thing she had achieved and that was to arouse Jake's awareness of her again, although now she refused to acknowledge him.

Choking over mouthfuls of a vegetable consommé, she asked herself why she had done such a thing. It had been an embarrassment to everybody, not least to herself, and she squirmed inside when she considered how Jake might react when they were alone together again. But, she told herself fiercely, she had had justification. After all, there had been no talk of marriage between Jake and herself, and he had had no right to leave her to be catechised by his mother while he ignored what was going on.

The consommé was followed by roast beef, and there was a lemon soufflé to finish which melted in the mouth. Ashley ate little, however. Her appetite had been depleted by the events preceding the meal and she noticed that Jake ate little, too.

She was relieved when the coffee stage was reached and they left the dining room to seek the more comfortable chairs in the huge lounge. This was a room Ashley had not seen before and she silently admired the cream velvet upholstery of the couches and armchairs, the long purple drapes at the windows and the cream carpet underfoot. She was looking up at an enormous painting of some horses hung above the exquisitely carved fireplace when she realised that someone was standing beside her and glancing sideways she encountered Sir James's quizzical countenance.

'Chiari,' he commented, nodding towards the painting. 'Have you heard of him?'

Ashley shook her head. 'I'm afraid not. I'm quite a Philistine when it comes to art.'

'But do you like it?'

'Oh, yes.' She smiled. 'I love pictures of animals. I wouldn't exactly say they made the best subjects, but their lines are so appealing—you can almost see the muscles rippling under the flesh.'

'Very good.' Sir James smiled. 'I like that. Muscles rippling under the flesh, eh? I must remember that.'

Ashley found herself relaxing a little. 'Thank you. But I'm sure you're just being kind.'

Sir James slanted her a look from beneath bushy brows. Although he was balding on top, there was an abundance of hair lower on his neck and in the heavy sideburns which grew down his cheeks.

'And don't you think it's about time somebody showed

you a little kindness here?' he asked her disconcertingly.

Ashley flushed. 'I don't know what you mean.'

'Of course you do. I know my wife. I know my daughters. I also know my son—although perhaps not so well.' He sighed. 'You must not let what Helen says upset you. She's got some bee in her bonnet about Jake jilting Barbara, but I say better now than after they're married.' He drew a thick cigar out of his top pocket and placed it between his teeth. 'Tell me, did you mean what you said? About not wanting to get married for years?'

'Ashley licked her dry lips. 'I don't know.'

'You just wanted to spike Helen's guns, was that it?'

'Something like that,' she admitted awkwardly.

'Sir James shook his head. 'Well, Ashley—I may call you Ashley, mayn't I?' And at her quick nod, he went on: 'I'd advise you to think very carefully before committing yourself. Oh——' he held up a hand, '—not because I have anything against you personally, but—well, I shouldn't like to see you get hurt, and I know my son well enough to know that he's hurt one or two women in his time. That's not to say he's not a good man—or could be with the right handling—but you'd have to be absolutely certain you were able to do it before making any decision.'

Ashley looked at him curiously. 'And don't you think I can?'

Sir James studied her upturned face for a long minute, and then he frowned. 'I don't know. I'm not sure what to think. I've never known Jake do anything so—so impulsive before. He and Barbara—well, they've known one another since they were children together. It's always been an accepted fact that one day they'd get married. And now this! Oh, Jake's had other girls, I'm not denying that, but it's never been anything serious, if you know what I mean.'

'I think I do.' Ashley nodded. 'So?'

'Well, you tell me. He's brought you here, hasn't he? Introduced you to his family. He's finished with poor old Barbara. I'd call that pretty serious, wouldn't you? At least so far as he's concerned.'

Ashley shivered. 'You could be right.'

Sir James looked down at her. 'You knew all this al-

138

ready, didn't you? I'd say you know my son pretty well yourself.' He half smiled. 'I'll say this—I've never known him so morose and bad-tempered—or lacking in appetite. Did you notice this evening? He scarcely touched his dinner.'

Ashley linked her fingers. 'It sounds so definite—from you.'

Sir James looked up at the painting again. 'Do you see that mare on the left of the picture? That's Sophia. Would you like to see her?'

Ashley's eyes widened. 'You own the horse?'

'Hmm. I bought her after I'd bought the painting. She's in foal at the moment, but she's still an exquisitely beautiful animal.'

Ashley spread her arms. 'I'd love to see her,' she exclaimed simply, and Sir James nodded.

'Good. You must come back tomorrow—in daylight—and we'll go down to the stables together. You can tell Mark I'm going to show you the horse.'

'What horse?'

Ashley had been unaware of anyone's approach, so wrapped up in what Sir James had been saying had she been, but now she half turned and encountered Jake's lean face, dark and brooding, and not a little impatient as he looked at both of them.

'Your—your father's going to take me to see one of his horses,' she said carefully. 'Sophia. The mare in the painting.'

'Really?' Jake regarded his father dourly. 'And when is this going to take place?'

'Tomorrow,' said Sir James firmly. 'You don't mind, do you, Jake? You can't keep this delightful female all to yourself all the time.'

Jake's eyes were cold as he looked down at Ashley. 'I have to to to to Leeds tomorrow, Father, as you very well know,' he stated bleakly.

'Does that matter?' Sir James seemed to be enjoying baiting his son. 'Your presence isn't essential, is it?'

Jake took a deep breath. 'And how is Ashley to get here?'

'I'll send a car for her.'

139

'She'll be at school.'

'On Saturday? I hardly think so, Jake.'

Jake's lips thinned. 'I see.'

'Oh, stop looking so boorish!' exclaimed his father shortly. 'She can stay for lunch, and then she'll be here when you get back. How's that?'

'Do I have any option?' Jake took Ashley's upper arm between his fingers in a grip that hurt. 'Come and have some coffee, Ashley. We have to be leaving soon.'

'Leaving?' Ashley was surprised.

'Leaving?' echoed his father. 'So soon?'

'I promised her aunt Ashley wouldn't be late back,' said Jake grimly, and that was the only explanation he gave.

As she drank her coffee, Ashley was aware of Jake's anger like a cloud about her, and when he rose indicating that she should do likewise, her legs felt curiously unready to take her weight.

She said goodbye to the other members of the family, smiling at Jennifer and giving Lady Seton and her younger daughter rather polite little grimaces, and then after bidding a warm goodbye to Sir James she accompanied Jake to the door. It was not until she was outside that she remembered she had not said goodbye to Gerald Sawyer, and mentioned this to Jake.

'He'll survive,' he growled ill-temperedly. 'Get in the car. You can't go back now.'

The Ferrari tore up the gravel of the drive as they turned and swept away at speed. Ashley ventured a tentative glimpse at her watch and was astonished to see that it was only a little after nine. Did Jake intend taking her straight home at this hour? Her heart sank. What an end to an imperfect evening!

CHAPTER TEN

ASHLEY paid little attention to her surroundings as they drove away and it was not until Jake got out of the car to open a gate and then close it again behind them that she realised he was not taking her directly back to the hotel. But she was loath to question him; his mood did not encourage curiosity and she sat in silence wondering where he was taking her. Once, when she thought she recognised her whereabouts, she thought he must be taking her to the stables to see the mare himself and thus thwart his father's plans, but that was not his intention. Lights glowed in the distance and presently she saw the cottage nestling among its copse of trees. He had brought her to the gamekeeper's cottage.

When the car stopped, Ashley heard the Labrador, Bess, barking. She had obviously heard the engine. Jake thrust open his door and then glanced at Ashley, his expression hidden in the gloom.

'Come on,' he directed, without making any explanation. 'Joe will have guessed who it is.'

Ashley hung back miserably, wondering why he had chosen the company of the gamekeeper in preference to his own family but unable to voice the query. 'Don't you think it's rather late——' she began uncomfortably, but Jake ignored her, getting out and slamming his door behind him.

She had no option but to get out, too, and she followed him up the path to the door with some misgivings. However, these were quickly dispelled when Joe opened the door.

'I thought it was you, boy,' he greeted Jake warmly. 'Come along in. And Ashley, too. How's that ankle of yours, lass?'

In the warmth of Joe's living room, Ashley assured him that she had had no more trouble with her ankle, and Joe ushered them both to the couch and went to put on the kettle. There was a delicious smell of soup, or stew, from a pan resting near the fire and Ashley wondered uncomfortably whether they had interrupted his supper.

On the couch she sat stiffly, her hands folded in her lap, and when Joe turned she thought she saw his eyebrows ascend in a rather speculative manner. Jake was sitting on the edge of the couch, his legs spread apart, his hands resting between, and it was obvious from their attitudes towards one another that all was not as it should be.

'So?' Joe broke the awkward silence which had fallen. 'You've been up the Hall?'

'Yes,' Jake nodded.

'I see.' Joe digested this. 'So you won't be hungry, then?'

'No, thank you,' Ashley answered him quickly, her throat constricted.

Jake sighed. 'Something smells good. What is it?'

'Just a little broth I've been cooking. D'you want some?'

Jake hesitated, and then he shrugged. 'Why not?'

Ashley looked at him fiercely. Would he take the old man's supper?

As though becoming aware of her scrutiny, Jake turned then and captured her gaze. 'What is it?' he queried. 'Do you think Joe hasn't enough for both of us? I assure you, he has.'

Ashley looked away. 'I'm not hungry, that's all.'

Joe rubbed his gnarled hands together. 'Well, Jake, the kettle's nearly boiling and the tea's in the pot. The dishes are on the tray, and there's bread if you want it. I'll leave you to it.'

'L-leave us?' stammered Ashley.

'Yes, lass. I'm away to my bed. It's getting on for ten o'clock, and I need my beauty sleep.' He chuckled. 'Now, don't you bother about washing up the dishes afterwards. I'll do them in the morning.'

Ashley looked at Jake, but he showed no surprise at Joe's sudden departure. 'Really,' she began uneasily, 'there's no need for you to go to bed.'

'Oh, but there is, lassie. I'm tired.' He patted her shoulder as he passed on his way to the door which opened on to

142

the staircase. 'Oh, by the way, Jake, you won't forget to let Bess out before you go, will you?'

Jake rose to his feet. 'Of course not, Joe. And—thanks.'

Joe merely grinned, and opening the stair door bade them both goodnight.

After the old man had made his way upstairs and the sounds of his moving about in the bedroom could be heard, Ashley rose too.

'I think it's time I was going, too,' she declared tremulously. 'As you told your father, you did promise Aunt Mona that I wouldn't be late.'

'Don't be silly.' Jake didn't look at her. He went to the saucepan containing the broth and lifted the lid. 'This smells delicious. You must try some.'

Ashley clenched her fists. 'Jake, I want to go home. If this is your usual practice, bringing girls here, I'd rather not know about it.'

Jake straightened. 'I do not bring *girls* here. I've never brought a girl before. However, I did warn Joe that *we* might be coming.'

Ashley sighed. 'Well, I don't want to stay.'

'Why?'

'You know why. Oh, why did you take me to meet your family? You didn't really want to. You regretted it the minute I got in the car.'

'That's not true.'

'Then what is true? That you ignored me, that you let your mother ask me question after question——'

'You must have expected something like that.'

'Yes, maybe. But I also expected your support.'

'My support?' Jake's nostrils flared impatiently. 'My God, Ashley, I've had my fill of being told what to do so far as you are concerned!'

'What do you mean?'

Jake tugged at the hair at the back of his neck. 'Don't you really know?'

'No.' Ashley was looking perturbed.

'You knew Mark spoke to me,' muttered Jake angrily.

'Yes. But—but what did he say?'

'What he actually said isn't important. The content is

143

that he considers you too young to know your own mind—an opinion which, I have learned this evening, is apparently shared by your aunt as well.'

'But——'

Ignoring her interruption, he went on: 'If you'd been like Karen—if you'd been swayed by the fact that my father is *Sir* James Seton, by my—social position, let us say—they might have accepted it. But as you appear not to be—have in fact voiced doubts about our association to them—they feel that any attraction you might have towards me—if it can be called such a thing—must only be transitory, a fixation towards an older man due to the unexpected loss of your father!'

'Jake!' Ashley stared at him in horror. 'Is this true?'

'I'm not in the habit of lying,' he returned brusquely. 'Now, shall we have some of this broth——'

'Jake!' Ashley's cry was agonised. 'Oh, Jake, I'm sorry!'

Jake turned away. 'Yes, so am I.' He went to the table where Joe had left a tray and two dishes and an uncut loaf of bread. 'At least try the broth. Joe will be most offended if you don't.'

Ashley stood motionless for several seconds and then she moved, going up behind him and sliding her arms round his waist from behind. His immediate stiffening was off-putting, but she refused to be diverted.

'Jake,' she murmured, resting her cheek against his back. 'Please don't be angry with me. If I've voiced any doubts about us, it's only because I want to be absolutely certain that—that what we're doing is right.'

Her fingers encountered the fastening of his shirt and on impulse she undid two buttons and slid her fingers inside next to the warm hardness of his stomach. It was a tantalising experience touching him like this, and she could tell by the increased tenor of his breathing that he was not unmoved by what she was doing.

But he moved abruptly away from her, turning and saying violently: 'I'm a man, Ashley, not a boy. If you want time to play around, then I suggest you find someone else.'

'Did I say I wanted to play around?' she protested.

'Not in so many words, no. But it's obvious, isn't it? You

144

said yourself you had no intention of getting married for years!'

'Oh, Jake!' Her hands moved appealingly. 'You must know that that wasn't—well, it was just bravado!'

Jake leant back against the table. 'I think it was meant to hurt me,' he said. 'Why did you want to hurt me, Ashley?'

'Oh, I didn't—at least, I just wanted to show you that you couldn't treat me as you did!'

'How did I treat you? I don't recall being cruel to you.'

'You—you let your mother say what she liked.'

'I was merely leaving you to form your own opinions—as I had been requested to do.'

'What's that supposed to mean?'

'Ashley, your aunt, and Mark too if it comes to that, wanted to be sure that you'd be free to make your own decisions. They realised that I could give you an entirely false impression of the way things really are. They asked me not to influence you, one way or the other, to allow you to form your own judgements. That's all I did.' His lips twisted. 'But what did you do, you silly little girl? You blew everything sky-high. You made an absolute fool of me!'

Ashley felt sick. 'Jake, I don't know what to say——'

'No, I don't suppose you do.' Jake straightened.

'But you've never—you've never mentioned marriage to me,' she cried defensively.

'Did I have to.'

'I—I think so.'

'Why? You knew how I felt about you. I was hardly likely to ditch Barbara if all I wanted from you was sex!'

'Jake!'

'It's the truth and you know it.' He ran a weary hand across his eyes. 'Maybe your aunt is right—maybe you are too young. One thing is certain—in spite of everything, your opinion of me hasn't changed, has it?'

'I don't understand——'

Jake shook his head. 'You don't trust me. No matter how I try, you still don't trust me.'

'I do. I do!'

'All right, then.' His eyes narrowed. 'Stay with me tonight.'

Ashley's cheeks blazed. 'You mean—here?'

'Where else?'

'I—I can't.'

'Why not? Don't you want to?' His eyes dropped disturbingly down the length of her body.

'It—it's not a question of what I want. My aunt—and uncle—they would never permit me——'

'Ring them. Tell them my mother has invited you to stay there overnight.'

'I—I couldn't.'

'As I said, you don't trust me.'

'I do trust you? Oh, Jake, what is it you want me to say? Will sleeping with you prove I trust you? I—I thought you respected me——'

'Oh, *God*!'

There was such a tone of self-loathing in his voice that her eyes were drawn to his face. But he did not look at her. Instead, he tightened the knot of his tie and glanced broodingly at the broth.

'Shall we go?' His voice was bleak. 'I don't have any appetite for food!'

Ashley had no option but to agree. He had opened the door and she walked miserably down the path while he attended to the dog's needs. Then he turned out the lights, locked the door and pushed Joe's key back through the letterbox.

He came to the car and got in without a word, and although she ached to plead with him her throat was choked with emotion. She glanced at her watch once as they approached the lights of town. It was only a little after ten o'clock. It didn't seem possible that that was all it was. It seemed hours since they had driven away from the Hall—hours since Jake had told her he thought her a silly, immature child!

She glanced tentatively at him. He was concentrating on his driving and seemed unaware of her presence, while she had never been so aware of him. She went over the events of the past few minutes again and again in her mind, wondering whether he had been serious when he had asked her to sleep with him. The curious thing was she felt no offence at his suggestion—only an aching longing, and she knew that had he behaved differently, had he enforced his will upon her, she would have responded gladly.

She wished in desperation that this evening had never been, that they could go back to the day before when she had been so happy. She had behaved stupidly—carelessly—and for what? Because she had been piqued—because she had childishly imagined he was neglecting her.

She drew a trembling breath. He was right. She was silly—and childish. But what now? What price her vain boasts of a career—of independence? What were they when compared to her feelings for Jake; for whatever else this evening had taught her it had revealed one certain thing—she was in love with him, hopelessly, desperately in love with him, and she knew nothing could compensate her for that.

He parked the car outside the Golden Lion, making no attempt to help her out, and she got out slowly, half expecting him to say something—anything! But he didn't. He leant across the passenger seat, closed the door after her and drove away without even giving her a chance to say goodnight.

The hotel was still noisy with the evening trade and Ashley stood in the hall, wishing desperately that she could just go up to her room. How could she tell Aunt Mona she had had a good time when she hadn't?

As though on cue, her aunt appeared at that moment, looking surprised when she saw her niece. 'Hello,' she exclaimed. 'Where have you come from?'

Ashley heaved a sigh. 'We just got back,' she managed.

'We? Where's Jake?'

'He—he's gone.'

Mona shrugged. 'Well? Did you enjoy yourself?'

Ashley stared at her, her lips moving wordlessly. Then she just burst into tears.

Mona was horrified. 'Ashley! What is it? What's wrong? Oh, heavens, Jake didn't—he didn't——'

'No, no, *no*! Nothing like that.' Ashley shook off her

aunt's comforting arms. 'We—we had a row, that's all. Do you mind if I go to bed?'

Mona hesitated. 'Did you meet his family?'

'Oh, yes, of course I met his family.' Ashley closed her eyes for a moment, calming herself. 'Aunt Mona, why did you think it was necessary to say anything to Jake—about—about me?'

Mona looked taken aback. 'Did he tell you I did?'

'As a matter of fact I asked him! Aunt Mona, I'm not a child! I do have some sense, you know.'

'Mona sighed. 'Ashley, what I said was that I thought you were a little young to get involved—seriously—with someone like Jake.'

'But why? Why? I'm not immature, am I?'

'Well, you're not experienced, are you?'

'What does that mean? Experienced? Do you think Karen is experienced, running around with a different boy every week? Is that what I'm lacking?'

'Ashley, don't get so upset! Karen—well, Karen's not like you. And she's two years older. Besides, if you've had a row just because I happened to give him a piece of advice, then it doesn't say much——'

'We didn't row about that!' exclaimed Ashley tearfully. 'Oh, Aunt Mona, what am I going to do?'

Mona looked round and seeing they were alone said: 'Come into the kitchen and have a cup of tea.'

Ashley hung back. 'I'd rather go to bed.'

'And cry your eyes out—I know. Come on. A cup of tea will do you good. Then you can go to bed and get some sleep!'

But Ashley did not sleep. She spent a restless night tossing and turning and awoke the next morning feeling terrible. She got up and dressed in purple trousers and a navy sweater and was washing the breakfast dishes when there was a knock at the outer door.

Her heart leapt. Was it Jake? She rushed to the door and then stood back in surprise at the sight of a man in chauffeur's uniform.

'Miss Calder?' he enquired politely.

'Yes,' Ashley still couldn't think who the man was.

'I'm Sir James Seton's chauffeur, miss. I understand Sir James is expecting you at the Hall.'

Sir James! Ashley put a hand to her lips. Of course. He had promised to send a car for her this morning to go to the Hall and see the mare, Sophia!

'But—but I'm not ready,' she stammered.

'I'll wait, miss.'

The chauffeur bowed his head politely and walked away, and Ashley closed the door leaning back against it weakly. She was still leaning there when Mark came into the kitchen and he looked at her in surprise.

'Who was that?' he asked.

'It was Sir James Seton's chauffeur,' murmured Ashley reluctantly.

'Sir James's chauffeur? Who—Parker?'

'If that's his name, yes.'

'What's he doing here?' Mark was astonished.

'He came for me. Sir—Sir James asked me to the Hall this morning. He—he has a mare in the stables he wants me to see—Sophia.'

'Sophia!' Mark shook his head. 'Yes, I know Sophia. But why is he showing her to you?'

'There—there's a painting in their lounge—it shows Sophia and two other horses.'

'The Chiari group, I know.' Mark frowned. 'And he offered to introduce you to Sophia? What about Jake? Is he not coming for you?'

Ashley's mouth felt dry. 'Jake's away today, I believe.'

'You believe? Don't you know?'

'No.' Ashley clenched her hands. 'Oh, Mark, if you must know Jake and I had a row last night. Now, please, I don't want to talk about it any more.'

Mona and her uncle were not unreasonably surprised to learn that Ashley was going to the Hall again.

'Aren't you afraid Jake will think you're running after him?' asked Mona practically.

'Jake's away,' replied Ashley, smoothing a colourless lip-lustre over her mouth. 'I—Sir James asked me for lunch, but I shan't stay. I—I expect I'll be back in an hour.'

'Why go if you don't really want to?' asked David im-

149

patiently. 'Ashley, you don't have to pander to the old man's wishes, you know.'

'I know that.' Ashley half smiled, pulling on her suede coat. 'But actually he was very nice to me, and I don't like letting him down.'

'All right.' Mona gave her a reassuring smile. 'And if Jake calls, I'll tell him he has competition.'

'No! No, don't do that.' Ashley was quite urgent, and not until she had spoken did she realise that her aunt had only been joking.

It was quite an experience riding in the back of the silver-grey Bentley through the streets of Bewford. The car attracted attention wherever it went and she wondered whether anyone recognised her in the back. Probably not. In the shadows she could have been either of Jake's sisters.

Sir James met her as the Bentley pulled up at the front door of the Hall, but he was not alone. His younger daughter was with him, and Ashley's nerves tightened as she stepped out on to the gravelled forecourt.

'Ashley! My dear!' Sir James shook her hand smilingly. 'I was beginning to wonder whether you'd refused to come after all.'

'I—I'd forgotten,' murmured Ashley apologetically. 'I wasn't ready when—when your chauffeur arrived.'

'Well, never mind. You're here now.' Sir James glanced sideways at his daughter. 'You've met Hilary, of course.'

'Yes.' Ashley managed a smile. 'Hello, Hilary.'

Hilary Seton sniffed. 'Hello,' she answered ungraciously. Then to her father, 'Can I go now?'

'Oh, yes.' Sir James nodded to his chauffeur and then said to Ashley: 'Hilary is going over to the Forrests'. She and Barbara play squash together.'

Ashley forced her face to remain composed. 'I see.'

But she was relieved. She had thought that Hilary was to accompany them to the stables.

After the Bentley had turned and driven away, Sir James indicated the paddock ahead of them. 'We'll go this way,' he said, and Ashley accompanied him through the gate and across the lush turf.

One of the mares cantered up to them and Sir James

found some sugar in his pocket and held it on the palm of his hands for the animal to nuzzle. Ashley was less easy in the animal's company. She wasn't as used to horses as Sir James and they seemed awfully big to her.

The stables, of course, she had visited before, and she remembered that last occasion with disturbing clarity. Jake had been engaged to Barbara then and they had ridden into the yard together, so handsome and confident.

Sophia was white, all white, with soft eyes and a gentle appearance. She seemed to take to Ashley, but that might have been because the girl had sugar lumps and an apple for her. Ashley rested her head against the horse's neck and realised for the first time how easy it would be to gain comfort from the undemanding devotion of an animal. Sophia's affections were given freely, and she asked no questions or expected anything in return.

Sir James watched Ashley closely, and when they left the stables, he said: 'What's happened?'

Ashley was surprised. 'Happened?' she echoed.

'Yes. You're different this morning. More emotional, somehow. Did my son do something last evening after leaving here?'

Ashley shrugged, brushing her hands together to rid them of traces of sugar. 'Of course not. I'm so glad you asked me here. I—I have enjoyed myself.'

Sir James frowned. 'You're talking as though you're on the point of leaving. My invitation was for lunch, too, remember?'

'I'm afraid that's impossible.'

'Why?'

'I promised my aunt and uncle I'd be back for lunch.'

'Phone them. Tell them you won't be. Besides, Jake will be back later. He's expecting to see you, isn't he?'

Ashley sighed. 'You might as well know—Jake and I had a row last night.'

'I guessed as much.' Sir James didn't sound surprised.

Ashley looked at him curiously. 'How could you?'

'Tell me, Ashley, do you love my son?'

Ashley hesitated, then she nodded. 'Very much.'

'Does he know?'

151

Ashley shook her head. 'He thinks I'm silly—and child-ish!'

'Does he?' Sir James sounded less than convinced. 'I suppose that's why he didn't go to bed last night—why I found him this morning, flat out in the chair, an empty bottle of cognac beside him!'

Ashley's lips parted. 'Do you mean that?'

'Of course I do. Dear God, Ashley, Jake's in love with you. There's no point in attempting to deny it. He's gone away this morning heavy-eyed and morose—in no mood to do any business for me! Can't you put him out of his misery?'

Ashley pressed her hands together. 'If only I could!'

'Well, it seems to me that only you can.'

'But—but last night—I mean, he said that I'd made a fool of him, that I'd blown everything sky-high!'

'I doubt very much whether he meant it. At any rate, when he arrived back here after taking you home, there was one hell of a row!'

'About—about me?'

'About the way you were treated—yes. Ashley, as I told you last night, my son is not the easiest man to understand. But you must know how he feels about you!'

'I think I'm beginning to,' she breathed, a sense of well-being warming her from inside. 'Oh, Sir James, I—I felt so awful when I came here this morning, and now—now——'

'Now what?' he prompted.

'Now, I think I love you, too,' she answered shyly, a smile tilting the corners of her mouth.

Sir James looked well pleased. 'So. Let's get back to the house for coffee, and afterwards you can telephone your relatives and tell them that I've insisted on you remaining here for lunch, right?'

'All right,' Ashley nodded, and there was a lightness in her step as they walked back to the Hall that not even the prospect of encountering Lady Seton again could dislodge.

Lunch was not quite the ordeal she had imagined. Hilary was not back, and Lady Seton had obviously been warned not to say anything unpleasant. She didn't unbend, she didn't address any comments directly to Ashley, but at least she didn't make the younger woman feel that she was an interloper.

Afterwards, Ashley was left to her own devices, and after examining the books on the shelves in the library, settled down with a copy of Tennyson's poems. Sir James had shown her into the library, and had then excused himself on business grounds, while Lady Seton went off to play golf. As there was no sign of either Hilary or Jennifer, Ashley was quite content to browse the hours away till Jake's return. She pictured his reactions when he found her there— she rehearsed what she would say to him—and then smiled when she realised that all she really had to do was show him that she loved him and tell him that she would marry him as soon as he could get a licence.

At four o'clock, a maid brought afternoon tea and the news that Sir James would join her in a quarter of an hour. Ashley poured tea for herself and nibbled at one of the delicate cucumber sandwiches provided. It was exactly the sort of afternoon tea one imagined was served in a place like Bewford Hall, and she was smiling to herself when Sir James came in.

'Hmm, this is nice,' he commented, viewing the attractive picture she made curled in one of the huge armchairs. 'Jake shouldn't be long now. I expected him back half an hour ago.'

Ashley poured him some tea. 'I expect he found there was more to do than he had expected,' she said. 'Er—cream and sugar?'

'Please. But don't tell Helen. When she's around I just have milk.'

It was very pleasant in the library with its long velvet curtains and the pine trees outside creating an illusion of greenery everywhere. After the noise and bustle of the hotel it was doubly relaxing and Ashley sighed contentedly.

Sir James looked her way. 'You're not worried, are you?'

'About meeting Jake, you mean? No. I—I can't wait for him to come.'

Sir James nodded approvingly. 'Good. Good.' He took out his watch and looked at it frowningly. 'Five o'clock. He should have been here an hour ago. Where the devil is he?'

By five-thirty, Ashley could feel every nerve in her body straining at the ends. Where was Jake? Why didn't he come? Surely he couldn't have found out she was here and decided not to return until she had left, could he?

Hilary returned home a few minutes later, the Bentley's arrival causing a surge of excitement, swiftly followed by a sense of despair. She looked questioningly at Ashley's and her father's anxious faces, and then said, without her usual maliciousness: 'What's wrong? Why are you both looking so worried?'

'Your brother hasn't got back yet,' replied her father quietly. 'Have you seen his car?'

Hilary hesitated, and for an awful moment Ashley thought she was about to say that he was at Barbara's. But then, after looking at her father, she shook her head. 'No,' she admitted frowningly. 'I haven't seen him since this morning. So what? It's only a quarter to six.'

'He should have been back before four,' stated Sir James forcefully. 'If he doesn't come soon I'm going to ring Hastings. Perhaps he was later leaving there than I thought.'

But even as he spoke the telephone began to ring and Hilary rushed across to answer it. 'This will be him, you'll see,' she declared scornfully. 'Shall I tell him his *girlfriend*'s here waiting for him?'

'Give that phone to me!' Sir James had reached her as she lifted the receiver and without a word she handed it to her father.

For a few moments neither Ashley nor Hilary saw any particular change in Sir James's face, but gradually, as whoever was speaking went on, his cheeks paled, and his mouth thinned, and he sought a chair as though his legs would not support him.

Ashley waited only a moment longer, and then she rushed to his side, going down on her knees, pressing one of his hands between both of hers. 'What is it? What is it?' she pleaded. 'Sir James, it's Jake, isn't it? What's happened? Is he hurt? Is he dead?'

Her heart was pounding, her blood was running thickly, sluggishly, through her veins, and she felt so sick she didn't know how she could stand it. She scarcely listened to what

154

Sir James was saying, but when he finally replaced the receiver, she looked up at him with tortured eyes.

'Jake's had an accident,' he said slowly, through bloodless lips. 'On the motorway, near Ripon. They've taken him to the infirmary nearby. He's not dead—or dying, please God! But he's very, very ill...'

CHAPTER ELEVEN

ASHLEY'S eighteenth birthday came and went almost unnoticed. She lived through those early days in an agony of self-recrimination, blaming herself for Jake's accident, for his state of mind which had caused him to take less care than usual. Her aunt and uncle pointed out that he had not been to blame, that another vehicle had swerved across the central reservation of the motorway and caused a pile-up, but Ashley was convinced that had Jake not been so tired he might have taken evasive action in time.

And it certainly seemed as though the Setons thought so too. Ashley still shrank at the memory of Hilary's accusations in the library at Bewford Hall immediately after Sir James had given them the terrible news.

In truth, Sir James himself had said nothing to her detriment, but he had not attempted to silence his younger daughter, and in a dazed way had instructed that Parker should take Ashley home.

Ashley had wanted to protest—she had wanted to stay, to go with them when they drove to the infirmary to see Jake, but of course she had not. Instead, she had gone back to the hotel, a pale, shattered replica of herself.

She had spent that evening huddled in a chair in the living room and nothing and no one could arouse her. She had telephoned the infirmary and been given the news that it was too soon yet to issue any bulletin on Mr. Seton, and in any case who was she? The family had instructed that no information was to be given to the press, and it would be advisable if she contacted Bewford Hall in future for news.

The following day, Ashley had telephoned the Hall, almost before anyone was about, and a maid had told her that Mr. Jake had had surgery the previous evening and that Sir James and Lady Seton were still at the hospital. This information had driven Ashley almost frantic, unable as she was to find out why he should have needed surgery, and she had spent the whole of that day in a terrible state of shock.

Eventually, of course, the strain of not eating, of living on her nerves, took its toll of her and by Monday evening she was in a state of collapse. Only then did her uncle telephone the Hall and insisted on being connected with Sir James. What passed between them, Ashley never found out, but at least her uncle had news when he came back to her.

'He's going to be all right,' he said heavily. 'But he has multiple injuries and God knows how long it will be before he's up and about again.'

Ashley was lying on the couch in the living room, her eyes red-rimmed and enormous in her pale face. 'Can I see him?' she begged tremulously. 'Did—did you ask?'

'Yes, I asked,' answered her uncle with a sigh. 'But Sir James thinks it might be better if you didn't see him at the moment. He's not a pretty sight——'

'Do you think I care?' Ashley propped herself up un-steadily. 'Uncle David, didn't you explain? Didn't you tell them that—that I'm sorry—desperately sorry?'

'Of course I did.' Her uncle perched on the edge of the couch beside her. 'Listen, Ashley, try to understand. At a time like this relatives have to have preference, surely you can see that.'

'But what if Jake wants to see me——'

'If he did, then—then I've no doubt they'd tell you.'

'You think he doesn't, is that it?'

'Well, you have to admit, Ashley, it's possible. You didn't exactly part on the best of terms, did you?'

Ashley caught her breath on a sob. 'No.'

David stroked the heavy hair, lying so lifelessly against her cheek. 'This won't do, you know, Ashley. You've got to pull yourself together. Jake's going to be all right. Accept that. Whatever is between you—well, no doubt that will be resolved in good time.'

Ashley nodded slowly. 'I—I suppose you're right.'

'I know I am.' David got up. 'Now, I suggest you get along to bed and I'll have either Mona or Karen bring you up a hot drink.'

Her family were unbearably kind to her. No one, not even Karen, reproached her for her weakness, and over

Easter weekend they all went out of their way to make things easier for her.

But then on Easter Sunday evening there was an unexpected visitor. She came late—after the doors of the small hotel were closed and they were having their final drink of the evening.

Ashley had been on the point of going up to bed. She had made a determined effort to appear relaxed all day, but the strain was beginning to tell and she longed for the solitude of her own bed, even though she would cry herself to sleep as she had done every night since the accident.

David went to answer the door and when he came back and Ashley saw who was with him, she let out a cry of fear. It was Jennifer, and to Ashley that could only mean one thing...

'What's happened?' she demanded in tortured tones. 'It's Jake, isn't it? Oh, God, he's not dead, is he?'

Jennifer looked compassionately at her, noticing Ashley's air of fragility, the hollow cheekbones, the haunted eyes, and then she came towards her determinedly and put her arms about her.

'No,' she murmured soothingly, 'no, he's not dead. He wants to see you!'

Ashley swallowed with difficulty. 'Why? Is—is he dying?'

Jennifer shook her head, albeit rather sadly. 'Let us hope not,' she replied, and now her voice was choked. 'No, Ashley, but he's had a relapse——'

'*Oh!*' Ashley's hands pressed in agony against her lips.

'—and he is asking for you,' finished Jennifer quietly. 'Will you come?'

'Will I come?' Ashley looked round desperately. 'Of course I'll come. Just let me get my coat.'

Her aunt shook her head anxiously. 'Are you taking her, Miss Seton?'

'Yes.'

'Does Sir James know?' That was Mark, his face curiously strained.

Jennifer hesitated, and then she nodded. 'Yes,' she said quietly, 'he knows.'

158

Ashley fumbled her feet into her shoes, pulled on the suede coat over the shirt and trousers she was wearing. She didn't bother with her hair—or with make-up. She just wanted to be going.

Jennifer, calm and elegant in silver sables, turned. 'Are you ready?'

Ashley nodded.

'Good. Then shall we go?'

The drive to the Chalfont Infirmary in Jennifer's small sports car was long and to Ashley agonisingly slow. But Jennifer was a careful driver, and she had no intention of ruining her brother's chances of survival by crashing with the one person he most needed to see.

On the journey the two girls spoke little, but as they neared the Infirmary, Jennifer said: 'I should tell you, Jake asked for you as soon as he recovered consciousness a week ago!'

'What?' Ashley stared at her profile disbelievingly. 'But —but why wasn't I told—why wasn't I permitted——'

'My mother refused to allow you to be involved——'

'But Sir James——'

'My father was in a state of shock. I've never known him so shattered by anything. He was in no state to stand up to my mother then. She's a very determined woman, Ashley.'

'But it was her son's life!' Ashley protested.

'No. Not then—not really. It's apparently quite common for a patient recovering consciousness after an accident to ask for someone they've known—sometimes years before. No one imagined it would make any difference to his eventual recovery. And—in fact, later in the week when he began to recognise voices, he never even mentioned your name.'

Ashley looked quickly at her. 'Recognise voices?' she echoed blankly. 'What do you mean?'

Jennifer glanced at her and then her fingers tightened on the wheel. 'His eyes were cut by flying glass. They're bandaged at the moment and of course he can't see anything.' She sighed. 'You must be prepared for a shock, Ashley. You mustn't be squeamish.'

Ashley clasped her hands tightly together. 'I'm not

squeamish,' she declared. Then: 'But about his eyes, Jennifer—are they very badly injured? Will his sight be impaired?'

Jennifer swung the car off the motorway and they followed a slip road until Ashley saw the sign for Chalfont. 'Why do you ask that?' Jennifer frowned.

'I'm just facing facts. I'm not a fool, Jennifer.'

'I never thought you were.' Jennifer shook her head. 'And we have to be prepared for that possibility.'

Ashley closed her eyes for a moment. To imagine Jake blinded did not bear thinking about.

'Does it matter?' Jennifer was asking now.

Ashley looked at her. 'Are you serious? Of course it matters.'

'In context, I suppose it does. But allied to other, more important considerations it's of small account. All that concerns me is that Jake should survive.'

Ashley caught her breath. 'Oh, yes,' she whispered unsteadily. That was what concerned her, too.

The room Jake was occupying at the Chalfont Infirmary was as comfortable as any hospital room could be, but without the flowers which filled it with colour during the day it maintained a clinical aura of anonymity. There was something chilling and impersonal about the narrow iron bed, the neatly folded pristine white sheets, the plain woven bedspread, the progress chart suspended from the rail. It was a feeling that was enhanced by the bottle of drip-feed which was hanging at the head of the bed, and which was attached, by the means of intrusive little tubes, to Jake's forearm.

Ashley hesitated in the doorway gathering her reserves of strength. She had an overwhelming desire to cry, but that would help no one, least of all Jake. Somehow she had to go through with this in a cool and confident manner. If she revealed her inner anxieties to him she could seriously prejudice his chances of recovery.

All the same, and in spite of Jennifer's warning, Jake's appearance had shocked her. The upper part of his head and face was swathed in bandages, and his nose and lips looked drawn and grey. He was wearing pyjamas, but above the top button she could see the beginnings of the plaster cast that swathed his chest, very white against his tanned skin, a hangover no doubt from one of his frequent trips abroad. His arms lay limply against the plain woven coverlet, his hands without animation.

A great surge of love and compassion swelled within her, and at a nod from the doctor who together with the Sister in charge of this ward had accompanied them to the bedside she stepped forward and covered one of Jake's hands with both of hers.

'Jake?' she began timidly. 'Jake, it's me, Ashley!'

She felt a lethargic response beneath her fingers, and she gathered his hand into hers, gripping it tightly. 'Jake! Jake! Oh, Jake, what have you done to yourself!'

Her voice almost broke, but she saw his lips move and her own emotions were held in check as he articulated slowly: 'Ash—Ashley!'

'Yes—yes, it's me!' she cried eagerly. 'I'm here.'

'Ashley!' He said the word again, his tongue probing his lips disbelievingly. 'Ashley—is it really you?'

'Yes, it's really me!' She lifted his hand and cradled it against her cheek. 'Can't you tell? Don't you know my voice by now?'

His hand suddenly assumed a life of its own. It moved exploringly over her cheek, her ear, her throat; then it moved back to her face again, lingering against her lips.

'Ashley!' he said, and there was a satisfied acceptance in the way he said it. 'It is you!'

His hand suddenly fell limply to the coverlet and his head seemed to drop to one side. Ashley was horrified, and she turned agonised eyes to the doctor, who came forward and drew her gently but firmly away from the bed.

'It's all right, Miss Calder,' he assured her calmly, but she hung back, protesting.

'Is he unconscious again——'

'Mr. Seton is asleep,' explained the Sister. 'Even the slightest exertion exhausts him at present.'

'Are you sure?' Ashley was not convinced.

'They're sure, Ashley,' said Jennifer, her own eyes rather moist at that moment.

'But will he wake——'

'Eventually.' The doctor gave a slight smile. 'I suggest you and Miss Seton go with Sister Lawson and she'll provide you with some tea. You can come back later.'

Ashley nodded a trifle dazedly. She was beginning to feel rather exhausted herself, and she realised it had been even more of a strain than she had thought. Her legs felt all weak and wobbly and she was quite glad when Sister Lawson took her arm and led her out of the room and across the corridor into her own small office. The office was infinitely more cheerful and friendly than the clinical room they had just left, with chintzy curtains and comfortable leather chairs.

A probationer provided them with a tray of tea and then Ashley asked how long they expected Jake to sleep.

'It's hard to say,' said Sister Lawson, frowning. 'It might be just a few minutes—it could be several hours. I suggest you remain here overnight.'

'Oh, yes, of course, if I may.' Ashley was eager. 'But could I just ring my—my relatives? They may be concerned about me.'

Jennifer looked surprised. 'They know where you are, Ashley. Surely they won't worry.' She shrugged. 'They've probably gone to bed.'

Knowing Aunt Mona as she did, Ashley felt certain that she at least would not be in bed. 'I'd really rather make sure,' she insisted.

'Very well.' Jennifer sat back in her chair, sipping her tea. 'Perhaps you're right. I expect I'd do the same in the circumstances.'

Aunt Mona was waiting for Ashley's call as Ashley had felt sure she would be and accepted that her niece would be staying at the hospital overnight. Right now Ashley could have wished that her aunt was nearer. Although she liked Jennifer and was grateful to her for telling her about Jake asking for her, she was not family, and at times like these a member of one's own family could be an enormous comfort.

Although Ashley and Jennifer were given beds in a side ward neither of them bothered to get undressed, and Ashley lay wakeful, alert to every sound from the room adjoining.

162

At about three o'clock, Sister Lawson came for her again, and when she entered Jake's room he must have heard her because he said: 'Ashley? Is that you?' in distressingly urgent tones.

Ashley rushed to the bed, flinging herself down on her knees beside it, pressing her face to his hand. 'Yes, I'm here,' she breathed. 'Oh, Jake, darling Jake, what a terrible shock you gave us!'

Jake's lips moved in the semblance of a smile. 'Yes, I did, didn't I?' His jaw tightened and he made an effort to pat the bed. 'Come—come up here. Sit beside me.'

Ashley scrambled to her feet and perched on the side of the bed, taking care not to jolt him, and he raised his arm and cupped the nape of her neck with his fingers, drawing her head down to his.

'I'm—I'm frightened I'll hurt you,' she whispered, holding back, but considering his weakness he exhibited an immense amount of determination.

'Just let me kiss you,' he said unsteadily, and she made no further protest, but supported herself with a hand on either side of his body.

His mouth was warm and it trembled against hers. She had never known him so vulnerable and the knowledge inspired a desire to do everything she could to help him get well again. Whatever his injuries she didn't care, and if—pray God it was not so—he should be blind, then she would be his eyes. But now was not the time to think things like that. They must just concentrate on inspiring a will to live inside him.

'I—I love you, Jake,' she murmured chokily, and she felt a shudder pass through him.

His hand tightened momentarily on hers, and there was a questioning tilt to his lips. 'Do you? Do you really?'

'Oh, yes,' she exclaimed vehemently. 'I think I always have.'

A few minutes later Sister Lawson came back to find that her patient had fallen asleep again, his cheek against Ashley's hand.

Ashley must have slept during the latter hours of the night because it was daylight when she opened her eyes again and she could hear a barely suppressed altercation going on in the corridor outside the side ward. Blinking, she slid off the bed, noticing that Jennifer's bed was unoccupied, and went to the door, opening it reluctantly. The voices were louder now, and a sense of apprehension gripped her. Jake's mother and father were standing in the corridor with Jennifer and it was Lady Seton's voice raised in anger which had apparently awoken her. When she saw Ashley, her face contorted with rage, and although Jennifer had not heard Ashley's approach she turned, guessing what had happened.

'Good morning, Ashley,' she greeted her with a strained smile. 'I'm sorry, did we wake you?'

Ashley licked her lips. 'I—I'm not sure. What time is it? My watch has stopped.'

Sir James drew out his heavy gold watch and examined it. 'It's a little after ten,' he advised her quietly, and Ashley was astounded.

'After ten?' she echoed. 'Oh—Jake? How—how is he?'

Her eyes darted appealingly to each of them in turn, but it was Jennifer who answered her. 'He's all right——'

'No thanks to you!' snapped Lady Seton grimly, directing her anger towards the younger girl. 'How—how dare you come here? How dare you interfere! If it hadn't been for you Jake would never have had this terrible accident!'

'That's not entirely true——' began Sir James, as though empowered to intervene, but his wife ignored him.

'You have no business here, Miss Calder! I should be glad if you would arrange to leave as soon as possible——'

'Mother!' That was Jennifer, her hands tightly clenched. 'Don't you realise? Ashley saved Jake's life——'

'Oh, what nonsense!'

'It's not nonsense. When I arrived here last evening they were on the point of telephoning you that Jake had had a relapse—that his chances weren't good——'

'And that's what you should have done!'

'What? And have Jake die——'

'Jake wouldn't have died,' hissed Lady Seton. 'I'd have seen to that. You took it upon yourself to go against my express wishes——'

'I had to.' Jennifer's voice was low and angry, but even so the sound carried in the tiled corridor.

Sister Lawson's door opened and she came out looking annoyed. 'Sir James, Lady Seton—I'm afraid I cannot have this kind of argument going on outside my patient's bedroom. He might well be awake and able to hear. I'm not suggesting he can hear what you are saying, but the antagonism in your voices must be evident. As Doctor Lindsay has already told you, your son is over the crisis. His condition is most definitely improving——'

'Is it? Oh, is it?' Ashley couldn't prevent the impulsive exclamation.

Jennifer nodded, turning to her. 'Yes. He's going to be all right.'

Ashley felt a surge of relief even while she sensed that other matters were most definitely not improving. Turning to Sir James, she said: 'Thank you for letting me come anyway. I—I was so glad——'

Sir James's face mirrored his confusion and Jennifer stepped forward quickly. 'My father didn't know, Ashley,' she confessed quietly. 'No one knew. I took it entirely upon my own judgement——'

'It was an unforgivable thing to do!' Lady Seton almost choked, and Ashley felt worse than ever.

She cast an appealing glance in Sister Lawson's direction and that woman seemed to come to a decision. 'I agree with Miss Seton,' she said determinedly. 'Without Miss Calder's assistance I doubt very much whether your son would be in the condition he is in today.'

Lady Seton snorted disbelievingly, but Sir James seemed less willing to dismiss Ashley's part in the proceedings. 'Maybe——' he said slowly. 'Maybe if you had asked me, Jennifer, I should have said go ahead.' He shook his head. 'We shall never know. But one thing I must say, Helen, is that we should be thanking Ashley, not raving at her.'

Lady Seton half turned away, shaking her head. 'When I think of what might have happened,' she exclaimed, in a taut voice. 'He could have been killed—*killed*! And why? Because some little hussy doesn't know which side her bread is buttered!'

'Helen! Being bitter doesn't help!'

Lady Seton took a deep breath. 'I can't help it.' She took out a handkerchief and touched her lips. 'So much trouble —so much trouble! And all since Jake took up with—with her! There's poor Barbara, eating her heart out——'

'I doubt that,' muttered Jennifer derisively.

'Hilary says she is.'

'Hilary would!'

Sister Lawson was beginning to look uncomfortable. 'Please—all of you,' she said. 'I don't think this is the time or place to discuss personalities——'

'No, that's right,' Sir James nodded. 'My dear,' this to his wife, 'let us just be grateful that Jake is going to be all right.'

Lady Seton sniffed into her handkerchief. 'But is he?'

'Of course he is.' Sister Lawson was impatient. 'Look, I suggest you all go along to the staff canteen. I'm sure you could get some coffee there——'

'Couldn't I see Jake?' asked Ashley, with temerity.

'No, you can't,' flared Lady Seton, her anger getting the better of her again. 'He's asleep, isn't he, Sister?'

Sister Lawson sighed. 'It's just as well he is, don't you think?' She gave Ashley a compassionate look. 'Perhaps later, Miss Calder.'

Ashley nodded, but an enormous sense of apprehension was weighing her down. Would they let her see him? Would they permit such a thing now that it appeared that Jake was on the mend? Sir James was sweet, but his wife domineered him, and Jennifer—well, Jennifer would do what was expedient. Just as last night when she had needed Ashley.

But perhaps she was being uncharitable. Perhaps she had judged them wrongly. Lady Seton was opposed to her seeing her son, but what if Jake asked for her? They would have to let her see him then, wouldn't they?

The canteen coffee was strong and bitter and although Ashley added two spoonfuls of sugar she couldn't drink it. Jennifer suggested she might like a bacon roll, but Ashley's stomach revolted at the idea. Food was the least of her needs at this moment. She listened to the others talking, every now and then drifting into thoughts of her own. But she was aware of the bitterness, from Lady Seton particularly, and now that the crisis was over in some small part from Jennifer, too. After all, it was only too easy to think that had Jake not been so disturbed by the row they had had that he had spent the whole night drowning his miseries things might have been different. And who was to dispute it? Not Jake himself, still so weak and helpless, probably totally ignorant of the actual events leading up to the crash.

At last Sir James rose to his feet and looked down at the others. 'It's almost eleven-thirty,' he said. 'Jake may be awake. I shall go and see. Jennifer, I think it would be best if you took Ashley home now. She needs a wash and probably a change of clothes. There's no point in all of us hanging about here.'

'Oh, but——' Ashley faltered, 'what if Jake asks for me?'

'Then you'll be told, of course,' said Sir James quietly. 'Well, Jennifer? Is that all right with you?'

Jennifer nodded and pulled on her driving gloves while Lady Seton sat staring into space. They all had a curiously unreal appearance to Ashley and although she opened her mouth to protest that she would rather stay where she was in spite of everything, no words would come. Instead, an aching blackness seemed to be impinging on the outer reaches of her eyes, creating a kind of tunnel vision where everything and everybody seemed distant and unreal. She could hear the faint sound of voices, but they didn't seem to be getting through to her, and when she saw Sir James coming towards her she blinked and tried to ward him off. But then the blackness became complete and she was hardly aware of sliding from her chair ...

Jennifer was kind on the homeward journey. Perhaps the fact that Ashley had fainted had brought it home to her that the younger girl was just as distressed about this affair as any one of Jake's family. In any event she assured her that she would keep in touch and delivered her to Aunt Mona's welcoming arms with consummate gentleness.

But Jennifer did not get in touch that day, or the next

day, nor indeed the day after that. Ashley was due to begin her work at the library on Wednesday of that week, but no one could have expected her to do so in the circumstances. She spent her time listening for the telephone, waiting for an unexpected caller, and when none came she quickly deteriorated into nervous fatigue.

The Suttons' doctor was sent for and he prescribed a drug which not only revived her appetite but also helped her to sleep. Even so, she was not fit for work at present and the library authorities were supplied with the necessary information by the doctor. Apart from helping her aunt and uncle about the hotel, Ashley did very little. Her books no longer had the power to distract her and she knew her aunt worried about the amount of television she was watching. But at least television was undemanding and it did help to speed the long hours.

There was an occasional write-up in the press giving details of Jake's progress, and she was relieved to read a couple of weeks later that he seemed to be making a rapid recovery. He was still in the infirmary, of course, but his family expected him to be home in four or five weeks. Ashley couldn't wait for that time to come. She was convinced that once Jake was home again he would send for her or she would make an especial effort to go to the Hall, and then——

But she didn't speculate beyond that point. She dared not. Time had reacted on her in a most disturbing way, and although she told herself over and over again that Jake loved her, that he had told her so, the words had a certain nebulous quality about them. As the days passed and no word was received from him or from any member of his family she began to have serious doubts about her own recollective abilities, and sometimes she woke in a sweat from a nightmare where she had convinced herself that it had all been a dream.

She plied Mark with questions every evening when he came home and in fact he did supply her with a constant report on Jake's health. Gossip was rife about the estate, but as yet there had been little talk about the broken engagement. Ashley sometimes wondered whether Barbara was kept in touch about Jake's improvement and whether she visited him. After all, she was a friend of the family, she had known Jake since they were children, and it was natural that she should be as concerned about him as anyone else. But such thoughts did not bear consideration, and Ashley strove not to think of how much easier it was to persuade a weakened man that his duty lay in following the wishes of his family.

Then one morning she couldn't find the daily paper. She spent several minutes searching for it, only to be told by her uncle that he had accidentally used it to mop up some beer in the bar. She hadn't suspected anything. It wasn't urgent that she should read the paper, although she usually did so, searching for any small item about the Setons. But when Jeff Saunders came that evening to call for Karen he had the *Despatch*, the evening counterpart of the *Echo*, and was only too willing to lend it to her.

And then she realised why the morning paper had so mysteriously disappeared. At the foot of the front page there was a picture of Jake, sitting up in bed at the infirmary, dark glasses hiding his eyes. But it was not Jake which had made her uncle destroy the morning paper—it was the woman seated so confidently beside him, Barbara St. John Forrest, and the caption read—*Sir James Seton's son, Jake, and his fiancée, Miss Barbara St. John Forrest, photographed in the Chalfont Infirmary where Mr. Seton is recovering from a car accident* . . .

CHAPTER TWELVE

'I WANT a thriller, Miss Calder! You know what I like, don't you?'

Miss Stewart smiled confidingly at Ashley and Ashley managed a smile in return. 'Yes, Miss Stewart,' she agreed dryly. 'You like plenty of dead bodies, don't you?'

Miss Stewart, an angelic-looking old lady in her early seventies, chuckled. 'Well, my dear, when you get to my age you'll realise that there's very little excitement in life except what you read in books.'

Ashley nodded and came round the counter to scan the shelves of crime novels. 'Here's one,' she announced, at last. '*Dead Eye of the Hurricane*. Does that appeal to you?'

Miss Stewart turned the book over, examining the fly-leaf. 'Hmm—this sounds exactly what I want,' she decided, handing it back to the girl. 'Stamp it for me, my dear.'

Ashley stamped the book and handed it over. 'I hope you enjoy it,' she said.

'I'm sure I shall. See you again on Thursday.' And Miss Stewart made her somewhat faltering way out of the library.

After she had gone, Ashley perched on the edge of a stool and began sorting the overdue tickets into order. It was not her most favourite occupation, but since coming to work at the library six weeks ago she had done almost everything ... from making the tea to cataloguing the new intake of books. This latter task had suited her best, but she had no real complaints. She had enjoyed the work and while she was here at the library she was able to put all thoughts of Jake to the back of her mind. The other girls she worked with had known nothing of her relationship with Jake Seton and consequently there were no grounds for gossip or speculation.

Sometimes she wondered how long she could go on like this, living in the same town as Jake, knowing the same people. At present it was easy—he was at home, it was true, but confined to his bed with a trained nurse in attendance—but once he was able to get up and about again, then the difficulties might come. She didn't think she could bear to stay and see him married to Barbara St. John Forrest, and all manner of wild schemes had run through her brain. It was too late now to think of university this year, but next year she might decide to try for a place. After all, lots of people took jobs for a year before entering university and she was young enough to create a whole new career for herself. But how was she to survive another fifteen months in Bewford without, at some time, running into the one person she could no longer bear to see?

It was eight weeks since that awful evening when she had seen Jake and Barbara's picture in the *Despatch*, eight weeks since the bottom dropped out of her world. For she was convinced that a newspaper would not print something that was not factual, not something like that about people living in the immediate vicinity, and Jake must have seen it himself—and yet he had done nothing to deny it. So it had to be true!

For a while after that night she had drifted into a state of complete depression, but then as time went by she began to accept that her behaviour was upsetting the rest of the family as well as herself. That was when she determined to put emotion aside and make a new life for herself. And it did get somewhat easier after she took up this job at the library. Everyone was so kind. They had heard she had had a nervous breakdown—brought on, they suspected, by swotting for examinations—and she soon became a popular member of the library staff, noted for her conscientious and patient regard for their customers. They were not to know that the fervour with which she attacked every task given to her was motivated by a desire to lose herself in her work.

Now she finished sorting the overdue cards and looked at the clock. It was a little after four, a quiet time in the library any day and most particularly on a Tuesday. There were only two old gentlemen sitting reading at a table in one corner, and they were regulars who used the library as a reading room.

The swing doors opened suddenly and a woman came in,

171

looking round expectantly. Ashley paled. It was Barbara St. John Forrest. Oh, *God*! she thought sickly, what did she want here? And why had she chosen today when her fellow assistant, Sheila, was off sick, and the Chief Librarian had left Ashley in charge?

Barbara was looking particularly beautiful today in a white two-piece suit of heavy linen, a red scarf knotted at her throat. She swung round on her high heels, and then saw Ashley, slim and nervous behind the counter.

With a flick of her hand against her skirt, she approached the counter, an unpleasant smile marring her exceptional good looks. 'Ah, so you're here,' she remarked, resting purple lacquered nails against the plain wooden surface. 'I'm so glad. I wanted to have a word with you.'

'You wish to join the library, Miss St. John Forrest?' Ashley managed to sound composed.

Barbara's lips twisted. 'Me?' She shook her head. 'My dear, what would I want to join a library for? I have far too many commitments to find time for reading!' The way she said it made it sound like a disease.

'Then I can't imagine why you want to see me,' said Ashley politely, fidgeting with some tickets which needed filing.

'Can't you? No, perhaps not,' Barbara shrugged. 'Is there nowhere we can talk? Privately, I mean.'

'I'm afraid not.' Ashley was suddenly glad Sheila wasn't present. 'I must stay here. I'm in charge this afternoon.'

Barbara glanced round, cast a disparaging look at the two occupants of the chairs beside the table and then turned back. 'Well, I suppose we are virtually alone, aren't we?'

'I'd be glad if you'd get to the point, Miss St. John Forrest. I have work to do——'

'Oh, have you?' Barbara's nails curved ominously. 'Well, when I tell you what I have to tell you, I doubt very much whether you'll feel like working.'

'What do you mean?' Ashley felt twinges of alarm threading along her veins.

'Are you aware that Jake is not going to recover his sight? That in all probability he'll be blind for the rest of his life?'

172

'*No!*'

Ashley was horrified. She stared at Barbara as if she couldn't believe her ears, and the older girl gave her a rather bored appraisal.

'Oh, please,' she said. 'Don't look so stricken. It's not the end of the world. Just because the Setons blame you for Jake's accident it doesn't mean that that's how it really is. I have an open mind myself.'

Ashley sought her stool, sinking down upon it weakly. 'Are—are you sure about this?' she asked urgently. 'I mean, is this definite?'

'How definite can these things be?' Barbara shrugged as though the subject bored her.

'And how—how is he taking it?'

'Jake? Oh, I think he's resigned to it by now.'

'But there are specialists—operations——'

'Do you think they haven't covered every possibility?'

'No. No, I suppose not.' Ashley rubbed a hand across her eyes. 'I can't believe it—Jake unable to see.'

'Yes. Appalling, isn't it?' Barbara wrinkled her nose.

'Appalling is hardly the word I should have used——'

But Barbara wasn't listening to her. 'Of course, I had to tell him—tell him straight that as far as we were concerned, I was through——'

'What do you mean?' Ashley's attention was riveted.

'Just what I say, my dear. I couldn't possibly consider marrying a *blind* man——'

Ashley was stunned. 'But you love Jake——'

'I admit, I am fond of him, very fond of him, as it happens, but I couldn't countenance spending the rest of my life running after an invalid——'

'But he wouldn't be an invalid. Blind people live normal lives——'

'Oh, yes.' Barbara was scathing. 'Well, I enjoy golfing, and skiing and riding ... They're hardly the occupations of a blind man.'

'You could find other occupations——'

'I don't want to find other occupations.' Barbara turned her attention on the other girl more fully. 'And if I were you I'd make sure I was out of Bewford before Jake is on

173

his feet again.'

'Why?' Ashley shivered. 'Why do you say that?'

'Have you no sense? Can't you see that when this news gets out—when it's revealed that you were responsible——'

'But you're deserting him!' declared Ashley unsteadily.

Barbara gave an impatient exclamation. 'What has that got to do with anything? I can afford to go away until all this blows over—you can't. For heaven's sake, can't you see that I'm right? Everyone in this town knows Jake—likes Jake. How do you think they'll feel when they discover the truth?'

'But why should they discover that—that I had anything to do with it——'

'Because Lady Seton will make sure they do!' said Barbara vehemently. 'You must know already how she feels about you——'

Ashley drew a deep breath. 'Is—is that all you have to say?'

Barbara regarded her contemptuously. 'It's all there is to say. Well, what are you going to do?' She paused, running her nails exploringly along a grain of wood in the counter. 'I don't know why I should, but I might be able to help you.'

'Help me?' Ashley was confused.

'Yes. Help you to find another post—similar to this one —but some miles from Bewford.'

'But why should you want to help me?' Ashley stared at her.

Barbara's cheeks showed a faint rose colour. 'I don't know why. Perhaps I feel sorry for you.'

Ashley pressed her lips together. 'Thank you, but I don't need your assistance.'

'Why not?'

'If I decide to do anything it will be to go to university.'

'But you can't be accepted this year. It's May already.'

'I know that. But there's always next September.'

'A year from now!' Barbara was impatient.

'Why not?' Ashley shrugged. 'I think I can put up with the situation till then——'

'You're a fool, do you know that!' Barbara was really

angry now. 'A fool!'

'Why should that matter to you?' Ashley was beginning to feel faintly suspicious of Barbara's motives now. Why should she come here and offer to help her in finding another job? Surely it would have been more in the nature of things for her to sit back and enjoy Ashley's vilification.

Now Barbara's fingers tortured her scarlet gloves. 'I don't know why,' she exclaimed maliciously. 'I might have known I was wasting my time trying to talk sense to someone like you!'

'I think you'd better go.' Ashley got up from her stool, albeit a little unsteadily, and gripped the edge of the counter. 'Whatever your reasons for coming here, I have to make my own decisions. If your visit was well meant—than thank you—but I really do have work to do now.'

Barbara's lips twisted. 'Well, don't get any ideas of playing the lady bountiful, will you? I heard of how Jake asked for you when he was first recovering in hospital—Jake told me himself. He—he laughed about it. But he isn't laughing now—he speaks of you with loathing!'

'Will you please go!' Ashley couldn't stand any more of this. In the six weeks she had been working at the library her system had begun to recover from the series of shocks it had had at the time of Jake's accident, but now, after only fifteen minutes in Barbara's presence, she felt as if she was back where she started from, and twice as vulnerable.

Apparently Barbara realised that the two elderly gentlemen seated at the far side of the room were becoming interested in her raised voice and without another word she flung herself across the room and the doors swung softly to behind her. Only then did Ashley sink down on to her stool again and shudder at the full weight of what the other girl had told her.

Jake was blind—he would never see again—never drive his sports car at speed, never play a round of golf, never go riding unless accompanied by a responsible adult ... How terrible—terrible! And it was all her fault—he thought that now, and his mother had thought it all along.

She didn't know how she got through the rest of the day, but when she arrived home Mona saw at once that something had happened. In a choked voice, Ashley poured out the whole story, and Mona listened in silence, for once unable to offer any panacea for the girl's misery.

'But *you* know it's not true,' she said at last. 'Heavens, in the newspaper it stated clearly that Jake was not to blame in any way for the accident. It was the car that came across the central area—it hit him broadside on!'

'I know that's what they said——'

'What do you mean, it's what they said? That's how it happened.'

Karen came in a few minutes later and looked at Ashley's tear-wet face with evident concern. 'Now what's happened?' she exclaimed.

Her mother briefly outlined Ashley's interview with Barbara, but Karen did not take it in the same way. 'And you believed her!' she declared, when her mother was finished, turning to Ashley.

'Why shouldn't she believe her?' exclaimed her mother. 'Isn't it true? Have you heard something, Karen?'

Ashley's hopes were lifted and then dashed moments later when Karen shook her head. 'No. But if you ask me there's more to this than meets the eye. Why would Barbara St. John Forrest take the trouble to go to the library to offer Ashley a job elsewhere when for weeks—months even—it's been obvious she hated the sight of her?'

Ashley looked up. 'I think she wanted to tell me about Jake's blindness. I think she wanted to make me squirm.'

'Yes, but why? I mean, why forewarn you of something, give you a chance to escape before the news breaks? It doesn't make sense.'

Mona frowned. 'There might be something in what you say, Karen. So why do you think she went to see Ashley?'

'I'm not sure. There is one possibility.'

'What's that?' Ashley was watching her cousin closely.

Karen shrugged. 'Jake may have thrown her out. He may have told her once and for all that he doesn't want to marry her. Maybe she's afraid that you two will get together again and she's getting her story in first. That way whatever happened you'd think he'd come to you on the rebound.' She paused. 'And of course this business about getting you out

176

of Bewford might be just to lay the way clear for her again.'

'But she said she wouldn't marry a blind man——'

'Are you kidding? Barbara Forrest would marry Jake if he was paralysed! She fancies herself as the next Lady Seton, and she's no chicken to be worrying about which coop she queens it in!'

Ashley smiled a tearful smile. 'Oh, Karen, you almost make me believe you.'

'Well, why don't you go and find out for yourself?'

'What?'

'You heard me. Go to the Hall and ask to see Jake. If he refuses to see you—well, at least you'll know. You won't constantly be wondering whether it was all just a pack of lies. And one thing's for certain, now that he's blind he won't come after you.'

'Why not?'

'Well, would you? Would you expect someone to want to tie themselves to a blind man?'

'But you just said——'

'About Barbara. I know. But that was different. You're not like Barbara, and Jake knows it.'

'As if I'd care whether he was blind or not,' breathed Ashley almost under her breath. 'I—I'd welcome the chance to look after him, to care for him. I—I love him!'

Karen turned to her mother, her own eyes pricking at her cousin's obvious sincerity. 'Well?' she said sniffing. 'Wouldn't you, Mum?'

'Mona hesitated. 'Go to the Hall, you mean? I don't know. Ashley could be hurt very badly if—if things are as Barbara says they are.'

'But isn't it better to be hurt once—badly—than to spend your whole life wondering . . .?'

'I suppose it might be.' Mona turned to Ashley. 'What do you think, love?'

Ashley rubbed her knuckles against her eyes. 'He'd never see me. He hates me.'

'How do you know?' Karen was impatient. 'How do you know anything? For goodness' sake, Ashley, you've moped about here for months. Get some life into you and go! What have you to lose?'

CHAPTER THIRTEEN

MARK took Ashley up to the Hall later in the day.

It was much against his better judgement. Unlike his mother and his sister he considered Ashley was taking too much upon herself, that she should wait and see developments before doing anything so reckless, but Ashley knew that this was because he cared for her and didn't want to see her hurt yet again.

He parked the Land-Rover on the gravelled forecourt and when Ashley got out, said: 'Do you want me to come with you?'

Ashley touched his hand, showing she appreciated his concern. 'No, not this time, Mark. But thank you.'

'I'll wait, then,' he muttered gruffly, and with an apologetic nod she got out of the vehicle.

She mounted the steps to the white door with some trepidation. She looked down at her attire of navy skirt and plain white blouse with some misgivings, but they had seemed suitable somehow. It was a mild evening and the cardigan she had worn thrown round her shoulders was left in the Land-Rover.

She rang the bell and waited. It seemed only seconds before the door was opened. Had the maid observed their arrival and been waiting for her ring?

'I—I'd like to see Mr. Jake Seton, please,' Ashley stated, forcing the words to come out clearly and not jumbled as they seemed in her head.

The maid paused. 'Who shall I say is calling, miss?'

Ashley was sure the maid knew her identity. She had served dinner on that disastrous evening when Ashley had come to the Hall. But now was not the time to bring that up.

'I'm Miss Calder,' she replied. 'May—may I come in?'

The maid stood aside unwillingly and Ashley stepped into the entrance hall. She waited there on the soft carpet while the maid disappeared into a room on her right. Where had she gone? thought Ashley uneasily. Who had she gone to inform? Certainly not Jake on the ground floor. He would be upstairs—in his bedroom. She wondered which room he occupied. Dare she dart up the stairs in the maid's absence and find his room for herself?

The opportunity passed. The maid came back. 'Will you come this way, Miss Calder?' she requested.

Ashley cast a last despairing look up the stairs and then accompanied the maid across the carpet and into what appeared to be a study. There were filing cabinets against the walls, a sturdy mahogany desk with a leather surface and seated behind the desk—Lady Seton.

Ashley's spirits plummeted. So she was not to be allowed to see Jake after all.

'Good evening, Miss Calder.' Lady Seton rose and indicated the chair opposite. 'Won't you sit down?'

'I'd like to see Jake, please,' said Ashley without preamble.

'So I hear.' Lady Seton remained standing also. 'Might I ask why?'

'Why?' Ashley made a helpless gesture. 'Because—because I want to see him. Does there have to be a reason?'

Lady Seton sighed. 'Couldn't you have waited until my son sought you out again?' she demanded, her voice rising a little.

Ashley frowned. 'Would he have done that? After—after the way you deliberately kept us apart?' She didn't know how she found the nerve to say such things, but somehow after what Karen had said—that she had nothing to lose— she felt better equipped to deal with the situation.

Lady Seton shook her head. 'Have you ever tried to see my side of this?' she asked. 'Jake is my only son. I love him dearly. I—I don't want him to throw his life away on a girl who once the novelty of having money wore off will seek her pleasures elsewhere!'

Ashley gasped. 'But—but I'm not like that!' she protested.

'Are you not? How do you know? How do you know how you'll feel in a year—five years from now?'

'Lady Seton, I love Jake. I—I'll never change. I—I just want to be with him—to share everything with him. I don't care if his father cuts us off without a penny. I can work. I can support us both.'

Lady Seton frowned. 'Support you both?' she repeated. 'Do you think a son of mine would allow that?'

'In—in the circumstances, he might have to.' Ashley turned away. 'Oh, look, I know you don't like me, that you blame me for—for what has happened, but—if I could I'd like to make up for that. I—I'll do anything!'

Lady Seton sank down into her chair. 'You defeat me,' she said slowly, heavily. 'My husband warned me that this would happen—that now—now Barbara has gone he would not be able to accept——' She broke off and Ashley felt a sense of compassion for her.

Leaning forward, her hands resting on the desk, she said quietly: 'I'm not like Barbara. It—it doesn't matter to me. I—I love Jake.'

Lady Seton gave her a curiously uncomprehending look and then shook her head as though the effort to think was too much for her.

'My husband will be back soon,' she said. 'He and Hilary are down at the stables with that blessed mare of his, Sophia. She foaled two days ago.'

Ashley straightened, her heart contracting. How long ago it seemed since that morning she had come to see the mare.

'What—what was it?' she asked, her eyes brightening infinitesimally. 'The foal, I mean?'

Lady Seton sighed. 'A colt.' She moved her hand towards a bell on the desk. 'Will you have something to drink, Miss Calder? A sherry perhaps—or some coffee?'

Ashley was astounded. Lady Seton offering her refreshment? It didn't make sense. And it certainly didn't tie in with what Barbara had said.

'I—I'd really rather see Jake,' she insisted quietly, and with a shrug Lady Seton acquiesced.

'Very well.' She pressed the bell. 'I'll have Mary take you up. But please remember—my son is still not a well man.'

'I—I'll remember.'

Following the maid Mary up the stairs, Ashley could hear her heart pounding rapidly. The sound was out of all proportion to the exercise being taken and she wondered whether Mary could hear it.

There was a rose-patterned carpet on the upper landing and several white panelled doors. The maid led the way to one of these and knocked tentatively.

Ashley heard Jake's harsh: 'Who is it?' and her heart almost stopped beating. He sounded so grim—so totally unlike the good-natured, attractive man she had known. Was this what being blind had done to him? Was Barbara right? Did he loathe her? In spite of what Lady Seton had intimated? Had his mother allowed her to come up here knowing that Jake would finish the job she had begun? Was it her way of achieving a victory? All these thoughts flashed through her mind, and then the maid thrust open the door and ushered her into the room.

'Miss Calder, sir,' she said politely, and went out closing the door behind her.

Ashley hovered uncertainly. She had expected Jake still to be in bed, but he was not. He was seated, in his dressing gown it was true, at the window, and at her moment of entry he had his back to her. But when the maid announced her name, he turned, and Ashley saw he was still wearing the dark glasses she had seen in that picture of him and Barbara which had caused her such misery at the time.

'Ashley?' he muttered harshly, almost as though he couldn't believe his ears. 'Ashley! What the devil are you doing here?'

Ashley took a step forward. 'Yes. Yes, it's me, Jake,' she began unevenly. 'How—how are you?'

In truth she was disturbed by his physical appearance. He was thin, much thinner than she remembered, and the planes of his face were more pronounced, his eyes deeper set between the long lashes. His tan had disappeared almost completely, and he looked pale and weary.

Ignoring her question, he snapped: 'I asked what you were doing here. I don't recall any invitation being issued.'

Ashley looked at him helplessly. Even behind the thick glasses his blind eyes had a penetrating quality, and she had the uncanny sensation that he could see her uncertainty. Taking a step forward, she said: 'Jake, I had to come.'

'Why? Why now? What has caused this change of heart?'

'Change of heart?' She was confused. 'I don't understand. I've had no change of heart.'

'Oh, I see. This is a duty visit. Well, it wasn't necessary. And you can tell Mark——'

'Mark had nothing to do with my coming. Oh, he brought me here, of course——'

'I know.'

'How do you know?'

He turned, bending his head. 'I think you'd better go. We have nothing more to say to one another.' He paused. 'Unless——' Her heart lifted and then fell again when she saw his scornful expression. 'Unless I thank you for satisfying the whim of a sick man by coming to his bedside. But quite frankly, it wasn't such a great favour you did me.'

'Jake!' Ashley was horrified. 'You don't mean that.'

He lifted his head. 'Why not?'

'Well, because—because you have everything to live for.' She hurried on, smitten by the way his lips twisted at her words. 'You have, you have! Just because—just because Barbara—that is—not everyone is like her. Not everyone would do—what she has done.'

Her voice broke, and she was glad he could not see her brushing the tears from her cheeks. But he must have heard the emotion in her voice, because he said: 'Now what are you talking about, you ridiculous child? What has Barbara done?'

Ashley shook her head. 'I don't want to talk about Barbara right now.' She moved a step nearer. 'Please, Jake, don't be angry with me. I—I know you blame me for the accident——'

Now anger brought colour to his cheeks and she was startled when he got suddenly to his feet and stood facing her, swaying slightly. 'Don't talk such utter rubbish,' he snapped violently. 'I don't blame anyone for the accident. The car that came across and hit me had gone out of control —there was nothing anyone could do. And if that's why you're here—to try and justify yourself, then it's not necessary. I absolve you from all blame.'

Ashley quivered. There was only a couple of feet between them now, but the gulf was as great as ever. She looked into his face, trying to penetrate the glasses, seeing the glimmer of his eyes beyond. It was incredible that he could no longer see her. Although perhaps it was just as well. She was finding it terribly difficult to control her facial muscles.

'I—I didn't come here because—because of that,' she went on, forcing herself to speak distinctly. 'I wanted to see you. If—if only to—to say—I'm sorry.'

'You're sorry?' Jake's jaw was taut. 'For what?'

'For—for everything——' she choked, and then gasped as his hands reached for her, catching her shoulders and drawing her inexorably towards him.

'Dear God, Ashley,' he groaned, against her neck, 'let me kiss you just once more...'

She raised her face in amazement, her eyes widening at the passion in his face—in his voice. His mouth on hers was as hard and hungry as ever, his lean body was reassuringly warm and demanding.

With a little sob she wound her arms round his neck and kissed him back, and when his mouth left hers to seek her neck and throat she pressed her lips to his cheek and his ear, murmuring softly to him as she did so.

It was as though they were starving for one another, and it was not until Jake staggered back, seeking his chair again, that she remembered he was not a well man. With an exclamation of concern, she went down on her knees beside his chair, pressing her lips to his hands, his fingers, putting his hands on her hair, caressing his thigh.

'Oh, Jake,' she breathed huskily, 'I love you, I love you, I love you...'

He lifted her chin then, and it was almost as though he was looking down into her face. 'You love me?' he demanded. 'I find that very hard to believe.'

'Why? Why?' Her eyes were unconsciously appealing. 'You must know it's true.'

Jake withdrew from her probing fingers. 'You don't know

183

what you're saying,' he muttered harshly. 'I don't need your sympathy—your pity!'

'Sympathy? Pity?' Ashley knelt before him. 'Jake, I loved you before you needed anyone's sympathy. I've told you, I'm not like Barbara. I—I wouldn't do what she has done.'

His eyes narrowed. 'And exactly what has she done?'

Ashley lifted her shoulders. 'You must know, Jake. However painful it is to you——'

'I know that Barbara and I are through—finally through. But you knew that months ago.'

Ashley bent her head. 'You don't have to pretend to me, Jake. I do read the papers. I saw what was going on. But I don't care now——'

Jake gritted his teeth. 'For God's sake, Ashley, get to the point!' he exclaimed, and she was concerned at his pallor.

'All right.' She drew a trembling breath. 'Barbara told me. She came to see me—to gloat, I think. But I didn't take it in the way she intended.'

'Take what?' He sounded deathly tired.

'Your—your blindness——'

'My what?' Now he was turning her way. She could swear he was looking at her. With trembling fingers he tore off the dark glasses and she saw his dilated pupils, the bruised sockets, but an unmistakable awareness as well. 'I'm not blind!' he bit out savagely. 'God, did she tell you I was?'

Ashley's lips were parted and she was nodding speechlessly.

Jake ran an unsteady hand through his hair. 'I'm not blind,' he repeated. 'My left eye was damaged, I admit, and it's still not completely recovered—hence the dark glasses. But I can see you as clearly as I ever could!'

'Oh, Jake!' The tears were running unheeded down Ashley's cheeks now, but they were tears of relief, not misery.

Jake calmed himself with difficulty and then, putting the dark glasses aside, bent forward to draw her between his legs. Articulating with evident difficulty, he said: 'You—came—here—thinking—I was blind?'

She nodded.

'For—for what purpose?'

'To tell you I didn't care. That I would be your eyes——'

Jake drew a deep breath. 'Tell me what else Barbara said.'

'She—she said—she had told you she couldn't marry you——'

'Because I was blind?'

Ashley nodded, again. 'Yes. I—she said everyone blamed me for the accident, that—that I should get out of Bewford before you were well again and everything came out——'

'The bitch!' Jake's voice was harsh. 'Well, let me tell you, Ashley, that Barbara and I were through long before this accident.' He sighed. 'I thought I'd convinced you of that.'

'But the picture—the picture in the paper——'

Jake smote his forehead. 'Of course! The picture with Barbara. Well, what of it?'

'The caption said she was your fiancée.'

'Did it?' Jake shook his head. 'I'm afraid I didn't care too much one way or the other then.' He looked down at her kneeling confidently between his legs. 'Is that why you didn't come to see me?'

Ashley bent her head. 'Partly.'

'And the rest?'

'Did you want to see me?'

Jake's expression darkened. 'That's a pointless question,' he muttered harshly. 'You must know I did.'

Suddenly everything was going to be all right. Ashley could hardly believe it. She looked up into his face and her heart was in her eyes.

'But no one told me,' she exclaimed. 'And—and your mother—every member of your family had made it plain that they considered me to blame——'

'I'm a member of my family, and I didn't blame you,' stated Jake huskily, his hands curving round the nape of her neck under her hair.

'I didn't know that.'

'No.' Jake looked down at her and there was a disturbing tenderness to his gaze. 'And you came here—expecting to find a blind man!' He shook his head disbelievingly. 'You would have married me—in spite of such a disability?'

Ashley flushed. 'Of course I would.'

'But what about your ideas of independence—a career?'

Ashley pressed her lips together tremulously. 'I've discovered I'm not so independent, after all.'

Jake pressed her closer to him and she slid her arms round his waist, resting her head against his chest. 'When I recovered—after the accident,' he went on, 'I asked for you—why didn't you come?'

Ashley shook her head. 'I wasn't told until a week later.'

Jake pressed her away, looking down at her searchingly. 'You mean no one let you know I needed you?'

Ashley shook her head once more.

'*My God!*' Jake gathered her close again. 'My mother has a lot to answer for. So how did you get to see me eventually?'

'Jennifer told me you were asking for me.'

'I see. She came for you, I suppose.'

'Yes.'

Jake nodded. She must have felt a sense of conscience. And maybe the fact that her fiancé died in a car accident had had something to do with it. She must have guessed how you would feel.' He sounded bitter. 'But my mother—I'm surprised she allowed it.'

'She didn't,' admitted Ashley. 'Jennifer made the decision without asking permission.'

'It's beginning to make sense.' Jake bent and touched his lips to her neck. 'Oh, Ashley, if you knew how often I've wanted to do this. I imagined everything was over between us. I used to wonder if you'd find somebody else while I was in hospital. At times I wanted to kill you——'

'Oh, Jake!'

'Yes. Primitive, isn't it?' Jake half smiled. 'But I love you so much . . .' He hesitated. 'But Barbara—well, that's something else.'

'Why should she do a thing like that?'

'I don't know. Unless she's realised finally that I mean what I say. That as far as she and I getting married is concerned, it's over.'

'She—she pretended she wanted to help me. She even offered to find me a job elsewhere.'

'The devil she did!' Jake's arms tightened about her. Then he gave a faint chuckle. 'I imagine she thought you would shy off at the first suggestion of disability—as no doubt she would have done.'

'Karen thought there was something suspicious about it.'

'As I've said before, your cousin is a very astute girl,' remarked Jake, and his voice was softening now. 'So—what do we do?'

Ashley drew back to look at him. 'What do you mean?'

'Well? I warn you, it may be months before I'm completely fit again, but—well, if you're willing, we could get married quite soon.'

'Oh, yes—yes, please.' Ashley was eager. Then she frowned. 'Mark will be wondering where I am.'

'Yes. He's outside, isn't he?'

'Of course. How did you know he brought me?'

'My windows overlook the forecourt,' replied Jake, with a smile. 'You've no idea how nervous I was when you came in. I couldn't imagine why you'd come.'

'And now?'

'Just try and get away.' Jake stroked her cheek, but there was a trace of his old arrogance in his voice. 'I'm not going to pretend that you'll find it easy to begin with—my mother needs time to adjust. But I promise you, we'll have a home of our own and you can do in it as you like. Does that sound reasonable?'

'It—it sounds like heaven,' confessed Ashley, her lips trembling.

'Hmm.' Jake's lips curved sensuously. 'And I think Mark will have to wait just a little while longer, don't you . . .?'

Harlequin Presents...

Take these 4 best-selling novels FREE

as advertised on TV

That's right! FOUR first-rate Harlequin romance novels by four world renowned authors, FREE, as your introduction to the Harlequin Presents Subscription Plan. Be swept along by these FOUR exciting, poignant and sophisticated novels . . . . Travel to the Mediterranean island of Cyprus in **Anne Hampson**'s "Gates of Steel" . . . to Portugal for **Anne Mather**'s "Sweet Revenge" . . . to France and **Violet Winspear**'s "Devil in a Silver Room" . . . and the sprawling state of Texas for **Janet Dailey**'s "No Quarter Asked."

Join the millions of avid Harlequin readers all over the world who delight in the magic of a really exciting novel. SIX great NEW titles published EACH MONTH! Each month you will get to know exciting, interesting, true-to-life people . . . . You'll be swept to distant lands you've dreamed of visiting . . . . Intrigue, adventure, romance, and the destiny of many lives will thrill you through each Harlequin Presents novel.

 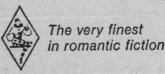

Harlequin Presents...

The very finest in romantic fiction

Get all the latest books before they're sold out!

As a Harlequin subscriber you actually receive your personal copies of the latest Presents novels immediately after they come off the press, so you're sure of getting all 6 each month.

Cancel your subscription whenever you wish!

You don't have to buy any minimum number of books. Whenever you decide to stop your subscription just let us know and we'll cancel all further shipments.

Your FREE gift includes

Sweet Revenge by **Anne Mather**
Devil in a Silver Room by **Violet Winspear**
Gates of Steel by **Anne Hampson**
No Quarter Asked by **Janet Dailey**

FREE Gift Certificate
and subscription reservation

Mail this coupon today!

In the U.S.A.
1440 South Priest Drive
Tempe, AZ 85281

In Canada
649 Ontario Street
Stratford, Ontario N5A 6W2

Harlequin Reader Service:

Please send me my 4 Harlequin Presents books free. Also, reserve a subscription to the 6 new Harlequin Presents novels published each month. Each month I will receive 6 new Presents novels at the low price of $1.75 each [*Total – $10.50 a month*]. There are no shipping and handling or any other hidden charges. I am free to cancel at any time, but even if I do, these first 4 books are still mine to keep absolutely FREE without any obligation.

NAME _____ (PLEASE PRINT)

ADDRESS _____

CITY _____ STATE / PROV. _____ ZIP / POSTAL CODE _____